LONGARM HAD THE NAGGING IDEA THAT HE HAD SEEN HENRY BAXTER BEFORE...

"This is Mr. Long, Daddy," Marianne was saying. "He's a United States marshal, and..."

Baxter's face went deathly pale. His expression changed from joy to ferocious anger and fear. His lips drew back into a snarling grimace like that of a cornered predator, and without warning he grabbed Marianne's shoulders and threw the girl against Longarm, tangling the two of them there in the hallway while Baxter bolted back into his room.

"Damn it!"

Marianne's squeal of shocked surprise went unheard by either man.

"Don't Baxter, *don't!*" the marshal ordered.

The man had reached the nightstand beside his bed. He grabbed up his revolver.

"Please don't," Longarm shouted.

But Henry Baxter was not listening, and Longarm had no other choice but to defend himself...

Also in the LONGARM series
from Jove

TABOR EVANS

LONGARM

AND THE DURANGO PAYROLL

A JOVE BOOK

LONGARM AND THE DURANGO PAYROLL

A Jove Book/published by arrangement with
the author

PRINTING HISTORY
Jove edition/February 1985

ISBN: 0-515-08109-4

Jove books are published by The Berkley Publishing Group,
200 Madison Avenue, New York, N.Y. 10016. The words
"A JOVE BOOK" and the "J" with sunburst are trademarks
belonging to Jove Publications, Inc.

PRINTED IN THE UNITED STATES OF AMERICA

LONGARM

AND THE
DURANGO PAYROLL

Chapter 1

Billy Vail looked serious. And, in fact, downright uncomfortable. He kept fiddling with an official-looking sheet of paper that was the only object in front of him on the broad surface of his office desk.

He had even offered Longarm a drink without having to be asked. Something was definitely chewing on the boss, Longarm thought. Something Billy Vail did not like. Something Longarm suspected he was about to have the opportunity to dislike as well.

Until now Deputy U. S. Marshal Custis Long had actually felt relieved to be summoned to the boss's office in the middle of the working day. He had spent the morning and the early part of the afternoon serving federal grand jury summonses, which he considered to be one of the most boring and time-consuming of all possible tasks, and so it had been with no small degree of pleasure that he had turned the chore over to Walt Frese and returned to the office in the federal building on Colfax. Now that sense of pleasure had been diluted by the marshal's obvious concern and discomfort.

Something Billy Vail did not like was going on here. And Billy was not a man who was easily spooked.

"What is it, Billy?" Longarm prompted, pouring a second tot of Maryland rye for himself and another glass of Madeira for his boss.

Vail sighed and rubbed an office-softened palm across the top of his balding pate. The pink-cheeked marshal was dragging his heels about getting into this one. That too was unlike him. Vail had been a first-rate field man himself before he was appointed to his present office, and he usually believed in going to the heart of things without hesitation. Today he seemed to be having more than a little difficulty with that old habit.

Eventually, in a voice Longarm thought sounded slow and uncertain, Vail said, "I want you to know, Custis, that you can refuse this job. I won't hold it against you or even put it into your record. I want you to know that."

A statement like that was damn near shocking when it came from a hard driver like Billy Vail. The man always operated on the principle that orders were to be obeyed and duties were to be honored.

It did not escape Longarm's attention either that the marshal had chosen to use his first name. No title and no comfortable nickname. Billy was truly fretted.

Longarm sat and crossed his legs. He deliberately took his time about flicking a speck of imaginary dust from the leather top of his stovepipe boot and taking a short nip of the belly-warming rye. He was wondering without much success what he could say or do to help put Billy at ease in this unusual situation, because Longarm genuinely liked the man in addition to respecting him.

"I can't say aye or nay, Billy, until I hear what the problem is," he said after a moment.

"Of course." Vail rubbed at his chin, then fiddled with the document again. Longarm idly noticed that, as always, the marshal looked freshly shaved, even though it was the middle of the afternoon and he could not possibly have just finished shaving. Longarm tried to remember if he had ever seen Billy Vail with stubble

2

on his cheeks. If so, he could not recall the occasion.

Eventually Vail's expression hardened, and he leaned forward to look Longarm direct in the eyes for the first time since his best deputy had entered the office. "This could be a suicide mission, Custis."

Oddly enough, Longarm felt a sense of relief. After all the hemming and hawing, they were finally going to get down to it.

"I'd go myself, Custis. Lord knows I *want* to. But Judge Hiram Knox has me tied up on this damn special commission of his, and he's ordered me to stay in town. Something about a group—bunch of damn political hacks, most likely—coming in from Washington tomorrow or the day after. I'm supposed to be here for the big event." Vail sighed again. "I spent an hour and a half over lunch arguing with the man, or trying to. Knox just isn't a man you can argue with. Hard-assed son of a bitch. Once he gets something in his head, you can't sway him. Even with the facts, I'm afraid."

That, too, was unlike Billy Vail. Longarm knew that everyone had certain private opinions, but Billy was usually careful to keep his to himself when it came to the people they had to work with in the service of their government.

As it happened, Longarm was in complete agreement with him about Knox. The man was a fool and had no business sitting on the federal judiciary. But then, no one had bothered to consult Deputy Custis Long when that particular appointment was made.

Vail blinked rapidly and went back to messing with the document on his desk for a moment. Better, Longarm thought, to let that momentary lapse pass by without comment. Longarm took another sip of his rye and concentrated on the flavor as it trickled down his throat while he waited for Billy to get back to the subject at hand.

"Like I said, Custis—" Vail tapped the document with a nicely manicured fingernail "—this could be a death warrant rather than what it purports to be."

He turned the paper around and slid it across the desk so Longarm could read it. The tall deputy had to lean forward to see it.

"An exhumation order, Billy? What's the big deal about a simple exhumation? I mean, if the guy is dead and all that, who the hell cares?"

"Read the name on that order, Custis."

Longarm did. "Oh." He sat back in the chair again. This time when he raised the glass of rye to his lips he did not sip but tossed the whole drink down. He felt like he needed it. And maybe several dozen more just like it.

Vail nodded. "The sovereign state of Colorado, in its wisdom, has asked that we go dig up the body of Chief Ouray." Vail shook his head with mingled anger and frustration. "The dumb bastards are asking us, just *asking* us, to start another war with the Ute nation."

"Look at it this way, Billy," Longarm said after half an hour or so of discussion. "If we don't do the damn digging, some yahoo is gonna sneak in there on a dark, cold night and dig the old boy up anyway. At least . . . well, I can *talk* to them, Billy. They'll listen to me. I don't expect them to like it, but it's the only hope we have to avoid another mess like that Meeker massacre and another all-out war with the Utes."

Vail nodded, but he still looked unhappy. "That's what I think too, Longarm." It was the first time today he had used Long's nickname, a fact which did not escape Longarm's attention.

"At least the Utes know and respect you. They respected Carson too, and if he wasn't dead I'd ask him to go with you. As it is . . . well, I just see this as our best hope, but a damn slim one. It still looks like a suicide mission, and I still want you to know that there won't be anything in your record if you decide to turn it down. Frankly, I wouldn't blame you a bit. This one, Longarm, I won't order you out on. This one you need to think about before you give me an answer."

Longarm gave his boss a crooked grin. "Just so I don't think on it too long, eh?"

Vail sighed. "Every hour that goes by increases the danger of an uprising," he agreed, "because every damned hour gives some damn fool down there time to think all the more about digging up that poor dead Indian and making himself rich."

Longarm did think about it while he crossed the room to pour himself another drink of Billy Vail's whiskey.

The problem was simple. Or not so simple, depending on the way a man chose to look at it.

The Utes were confined these days on the Los Pinos Agency down in the southwestern corner of the state. All of them had been moved there and the White River Agency closed after the disastrous outbreak a year or so before and its subsequent panic and loss of life, both red and white.

Near the agency was the town of Gray Rock. Billy said it was another mining camp, and Longarm was willing to take the boss's word about that. He had never heard of Gray Rock until today.

A few days earlier a gang of well-armed but apparently not extraordinarily bright old boys had decided to hold up the Gray Rock Bank. They gunned down the bank's teller and president and thoroughly pistol-whipped the vice president, then made off with a tidy sum from the bank's vault.

So far so good, but from that point on their luck had gone downhill in a hurry.

They were seen coming out of the bank, and in Gray Rock they were not dealing with a bunch of meek and mild city folk. The local boys were hard men, making it in a hard country, and when they saw a bunch of yokels trying to take the money out of their bank they didn't wait to holler for the law. They just dragged iron and started shooting. Afterward they had occasion to hold a hasty funeral for three of the gang members.

The rest of the bunch managed to get out of town, but they were hardly home free.

The town marshal telegraphed ahead to the agency police at Los Pinos while some of the more enterprising locals tore off in hot pursuit, and the gang was caught with Ute police in front of them and a posse behind them.

The Ute police had killed one of the robbers and wounded another, according to information received in Denver.

They managed to escape again by going through a section of the reservation that the Utes held to be sacred and inviolable even by white posses in pursuit of thieves. The Indians would not go into the burial ground themselves and stopped the angry posse men at gunpoint to keep them from staying on the trail of the gang. That right there, apparently, had come close to starting another Ute war, but eventually the posse had turned back after nothing more serious than some name-calling and one minor fistfight.

The gang members probably thought they were safe at that point, but the Utes at Los Pinos knew how to

6

use a telegraph too, and when the gang emerged onto the Jicarilla Apache reserve to the south they were met by still more Indian police.

This time the gang was not expecting trouble, and the Apache police wiped them out. The exact details were sketchy and were likely to remain so, but apparently there would have been a survivor or two except that the Apaches allowed their women to finish the job their bullets had started. So at this point there were no survivors of the bank-robbing crowd.

That should have been that, except that there was no trace found of the money missing from the Gray Rock Bank.

Both Indian and white trackers had by now been over every inch of the route the gang had taken. The robbers had been more interested in speed than in hiding their trail. But no one could find any place where the ground had been disturbed or where the money could have been hidden except in the freshly disturbed earth of old Chief Ouray's grave.

The only logical conclusion to draw was that the gang members had buried their loot there, thinking the gravesite would be the safest place possible for them to hide the money until they could come back for it.

And now some greedy idiot was damn well certain to think he could make himself rich by digging up Ouray, and starting a war.

Longarm sighed. With this particular problem ahead, sighing was an easily acquired habit. No wonder Billy Vail was doing so much of it.

"I don't suppose," he speculated aloud, "that we could wiggle out of this on a jurisdictional technicality. I mean, bank robbery ain't exactly a federal crime. Could we throw it back onto the state?" Longarm hated to weasel but, damn it, he thought they at least ought to discuss the possibility.

Vail shook his head. "I've already thought of that one, Longarm. The thing is, those Utes at Los Pinos are wards of the federal government, not the state. That's where our problem is: with the Utes and that exhumation order, which the state has already thoughtfully obtained. Besides, as you said yourself, if we duck it, then sure as the sun rises in the east, some moron is going to do the digging for us. Then we'll have the war anyway. Like it or not, Longarm, the job is ours."

"Just so you know I don't like it."

It was Vail's turn to sigh. "I don't like it either." The marshal thought for a moment. "I can get you formal authority to command assistance from the military if you need it. It might make a difference when you get to the actual digging if there's a company of infantry with Springfields and bayonets standing behind you."

Longarm grunted. "It might keep them from lifting my scalp right there on the spot, but that's about all it would do. Every white man for two hundred miles around would be in for it if we do it the hard-ass way, Billy."

Vail sighed again. "I know that, Longarm. But, damn it, I don't want this to be a suicide mission."

Longarm grinned. "I would have to say, Billy, that you don't want that a bit more'n I do."

"I'll get you that authority, Longarm. In writing. Whether you choose to use it or not will be up to your discretion."

"Discretion," Longarm mused. "Good word. I think I'm gonna need some of that."

"Uh-huh." Vail paused. "You never have said if

you are willing to take the assignment."

This time it was Longarm who sighed. "I don't think I have a whole hell of a lot of choice, Billy. Either I take it and probably get myself killed, or I don't take it and a whole bunch of other people, red ones and white ones, get themselves killed."

"Well?"

Longarm nodded. "Reckon I got to take it, Billy."

Chapter 2

The train clattered and bumped over an uneven stretch of roadbed. The ride was too rough for comfortable reading, so Longarm laid aside the newspaper he had bought from the boy back in Denver, many miles and many hours behind now.

He looked to his right and recognized the Buffalo Peaks. That meant they were beginning the long, winding descent down Trout Creek Pass. Another half hour or so and the comfortable part of this trip would be over. Then he would have to change to a coach for the rest of the long journey down to Gray Rock.

The angle of the roadbed changed, and the clanky puffer began to gather speed as it pulled them downhill.

Several seats away toward the front of the crowded car, a young woman rose and began looking uncertainly around the passenger car. She looked embarrassed, her cheeks blushing bright red. She seemed to be making something of a point of not looking at the man she had been seated beside.

Longarm gave her a casual glance. He had entered the car from the other end, and she had already been sitting there, so until now he had seen nothing of her but the top of her head protruding above the grimy seat on the Denver, South Park and Pacific coach.

What he saw now was ordinary enough. She was young—late teens or early twenties, he thought—and perhaps a shade plumper than he liked. Other than

10

that she was about as average and ordinary as a girl could be, neither plug-ugly nor exceptionally pretty. Just another traveler.

She did seem a little distressed, though. She kept looking up and down the length of the coach. The train lurched sideways as the car passed over a slightly sunken rail, and she had to grab onto the backs of the seats on both sides of the aisle to keep from falling down.

She steadied herself and began walking uncertainly toward the back of the car.

The train lurched again, and Longarm reached up to grab her wrist and steady her.

"Thank you." Her voice was low and nervous, and only the force of long habit tugged a hint of a polite smile at the corners of her lips.

"Of course, ma'am." She had her balance now. Longarm released her wrist and touched the brim of his flat-crowned brown Stetson.

He expected her to go on, but she stood there. He looked up at her again and could clearly see the concern on her face.

"Are you all right, ma'am?" he asked.

"Yes, I . . ." She paused, then shook her head. This time her smile was real if still faint. "No, I'm not. Not really. Is that seat beside you taken, sir?"

Longarm was surprised by the question. He had assumed, mistakenly, it appeared, that she was traveling with the gentleman she had been sitting with for all this time. "No, ma'am. Would you prefer to sit here?"

"If it wouldn't be a bother."

"Of course not. Window or aisle?" he asked.

"You wouldn't mind if I took the window seat?"

Longarm removed the newspaper he had dropped

11

onto the seat beside him and stood to allow her to pass without having to squeeze by him.

The girl sat with obvious relief, and Longarm resumed his seat.

Once she was trapped into the seat beside him the girl gave him an uneasy glance. "You don't . . . happen to run a saloon . . . or anything, do you?"

Longarm smiled at her. "No, ma'am."

"Thank goodness," she said with real relief. "And it is miss, not ma'am, if you please."

"Of course, miss." Longarm touched his hat to her again.

Apparently recovered now from whatever ordeal she had just gone through—or thought she had just gone through—she visibly relaxed. "I am Miss Marianne Baxter. Recently of Providence, Rhode Island. And you are . . . ?"

"Custis Long, Miss Baxter. Of Denver, Colorado, more or less."

"More or less?"

"I travel."

"I see. And what is it that you do, Mr. Long?" she asked.

Longarm hesitated. He had no particular reason not to tell her anything she might wish to know. On the other hand, he was not overly fond of being questioned by total strangers, female or otherwise.

"The reason I ask, Mr. Long, is because of my recent experience with that . . . uh . . . *gentleman* in the seat up ahead." She made a face. "He says he operates a saloon in some dreadful-sounding camp called Leadville. He tried to *employ* me." She shuddered. "It all sounded perfectly *indecent*."

"Yes, ma'am—I mean miss." Longarm admitted to his occupation, and the girl brightened.

"Why, *Marshal*. I could not have *chosen* a more trustworthy seating companion. Could I?" She smiled. She looked almost pretty when she smiled.

Longarm thought she was overdoing the breathlessness a bit. But then she had probably never been out of Providence, Rhode Island before. She was likely damn well frightened by the strangeness of her surroundings and was trying to cover her fear by gushing confidences to strangers. Which also, he thought, was what had probably got her into trouble with the gentleman up ahead. Very few men in this country were rude enough—or stupid enough—to be pushy with ladies they did not know well.

"I think you will find," he said, "that folks won't bother you out here any more than you want to be bothered."

"Do you really think so?"

"Westerners generally aren't much for asking questions. Or for answering them."

She made a face again that might have been taken for a pout, but after a moment she said, "That was a hint, wasn't it, Marshal Long?"

"Deputy Long, Miss Baxter, but most call me Longarm. You can if you like." That was an answer, if not one relating to her question. The girl might be nervous, he thought, but she was not entirely stupid.

"Is this your first trip West, Miss Baxter?" he asked. Actually he would have been quite content to spend the rest of his time on the train reading his newspaper, but the girl seemed to need someone to talk to. It looked like Longarm was the one appointed for the duty.

"Does it show that badly?" she asked.

Longarm laughed. "Not really. I was just making conversation."

13

"Your answer was very gallant, Marshal, and I thank you. As a matter of fact, this is my first trip away from home." A flicker of sadness crossed her face. "What used to be home, I should say."

"I'm sorry," Longarm responded automatically, although he still had no idea what it was he was expected to be sorry about.

"What? Oh. It wasn't anything *serious*, Marshal. Not like a death in the family or anything like that. In fact, it may be for the best. I may gain a family . . . a real family, that is . . . for the first time ever."

Longarm had no idea what this girl was saying, but he was determined to be polite. "Really?"

"I do have you confused, don't I?" the girl nattered on. "It is really quite simple. My mother died just *ages* ago. I don't remember a thing about her. And my daddy couldn't take care of me himself. So he put me into a boarding school back home in Providence. The school is just about the only home I can remember, although the sisters told me we used to have a really lovely home. They even showed it to me, where my family used to live. It was lovely. Just what a home ought to be. But Daddy sold it when he put me in school, and he came West. That was just ages ago, you see. And I haven't seen him since, although he never forgot to send money for my care. And he wrote to me once in a while. He was very good about that." Longarm got the impression from the rather forced tone when she said that that Daddy had not written nearly as often as Miss Marianne Baxter would have wished. But she was not going to admit that to a stranger, and probably not to herself either.

"Anyway," she continued, "I graduated high school this past spring, and they let me stay on for a time. But it came to the point where I would either have to leave or take holy vows. We talked it over and agreed that I don't have a calling for holy vows. And since I haven't anywhere *else* to go...well, here I am." She acted as if that explained everything.

"Why here?"

"Why...? Oh. Because the last letter Daddy sent was from out here. A city called Durango."

Longarm suppressed a smile. To call Durango a city was stretching things, even if it was the closest that part of the state could come to boasting a city-sized gathering of buildings and people to put into them.

"I don't know what you might be expecting, Miss Baxter, but I hope it isn't Providence, Rhode Island with mountains. I'm familiar with Durango, and it's not much different from Leadville. Which I believe you said sounded dreadful."

"Really? Oh."

"Don't be worried about it. You'll find that people can be mighty nice there. There just aren't so many of them. And I'm sure it will be a great pleasure for you to see your father after all these years."

She smiled. "I *am* looking forward to that."

"Of course you are." He hesitated, but his duty in the matter seemed clear enough. "If it will make you feel any better, Miss Baxter, I happen to be traveling through Durango on my way south. I'll be glad to see that no harm comes to you until you reach your father."

Chapter 3

Longarm wanted to travel on through the night. He knew that the longer it took him to reach Gray Rock, the more liklihood there was that someone was going to start a war with the Ute nation. But, damn it, there were no stages leaving Buena Vista until daybreak in either of the two directions he could have taken to reach his destination.

That was probably logical enough, he knew, because of the passes that would have to be crossed regardless of which way one went to reach the southwestern part of the state. But the delay rankled.

He even thought about hiring a horse and going on alone with apologies to Miss Baxter. But that would not have gained him anything. A stagecoach, with its relays of fresh horses waiting on the roads ahead and the ability to travel day and night where conditions allowed, would overtake and soon pass any horseman riding alone. So he seemed to have no choice but to lay over for the night in Buena Vista and head out again come morning.

Since she seemed to be a girl of some quality, Longarm was surprised to find that Marianne Baxter was traveling with a single suitcase, and that none too large.

He could have managed her bag and his easily enough without help, but he had to carry his McClellan saddle and Winchester too, and long habit made him reluctant to burden his gun hand. A dime and a smile, though, gave him a choice of several teenage loiterers at the station who were anxious to help, and as soon as the baggage car was opened he led a regular procession away from the depot, Miss Marianne Baxter on his arm and a kid named Tommy coming along behind with the bags and saddle.

"Where would you suggest we go, Tommy?" Longarm asked over his shoulder.

"For a room, you mean, mister?"

"Uh-huh."

"Ain't much choice," the boy said. "Town's pretty full up with the railroad buildin' on ahead and everything. 'Bout the only place that might have rooms to let would be the Grand. An' that's only because it's so expensive."

"Since you know where we're going, son, you lead."

"Yes, sir." The kid grinned and trotted around them on the board sidewalk to show the way.

The Grand Hotel was not necessarily misnamed—it looked nice enough for anyone's taste—but the boy had certainly been right about its prices. The snobbish young pup who was clerking there wanted four dollars a night for a room. As if it made any difference, he stressed that the outrageous price included a tub and bath water.

"That's too much," Longarm protested.

The clerk shrugged. "Suit yourself, mister. It makes no never-mind to me."

Longarm stepped aside and let another customer register. He groaned when he heard the man pay up without a whimper and tell the clerk, "Sure glad to find this room, man. I been to every other place in town, includin' the boardin' houses, and this is all that's left."

"I guess that answers that," Longarm whispered to his new companion.

"But the price!" she protested.

"It's that or sleep on a bench at the depot."

"He did say it includes a bath, I believe."

Longarm nodded. So did Miss Baxter. Longarm stepped back up to the counter. Behind him another man came in and got into line behind Longarm. Longarm recognized the fellow from the passenger car.

"We'll take two rooms," Longarm told the clerk.

The clerk's lower lip twisted into something so close to a sneer that he was fortunate there was a lady present or Longarm might have been tempted to wrap his tongue around his throat for a necktie. "One room left. Take it or leave it."

Longarm swallowed his anger, although that took some doing. "We'll take it." He paid the man quickly, before the fellow next in line got his money down first.

"Sorry," he told Miss Baxter. "You can have the room, of course. I'll sleep at the train station and come to fetch you in the morning."

"I couldn't have you do that, Marshal. I . . . may I be honest with you?"

Longarm led her a few steps away from the counter and watched all of their luggage disappear up the stairs. At least the place did seem to give service to match the prices.

"You wanted to say something?" he asked.

Miss Baxter nodded. "I . . . haven't much money, Marshal. Very little, in fact. I can't afford to pay such a rate."

"I see." Inwardly he was regretting the impulse that had made him offer to help this girl. It looked now like it was leading to a touch, just a small loan to "tide her over," as the saying would go.

"What I was thinking," she said instead, "was that we could, well, *share* the room." She blushed.

A girl who blushed so easily as that was not making any suggestions, he thought. She was just trying to promote a place to sleep for the night. Probably had never in her life spent a night without a soft bed unless it was on the train ride out here, and even then she'd likely taken a sleeper.

Longarm resigned himself to a night without comfort in a room that he—well, the United States government—was paying for. But, what the hell, he had certainly spent many a night under worse conditions than just having to be polite around a female stranger. "All right."

They ate at the hotel restaurant first, a light meal because the restaurant was as expensive as the hotel, and the girl insisted on paying for her own meal. Then they went upstairs to the room they had been given.

There was only one bed in the large room. The fact that it was a large one made little difference under the circumstances. Longarm's saddle had been set on the floor, and both bags were on the foot of the bed. Longarm moved his carpetbag to the floor at the foot of the bed and laid a spare quilt down there.

"I can sleep here, Miss Baxter. And since I assume you would like to bathe, I'll go down and have a drink. I'll tell the clerk to send the tub and water right away and take my time. When you're done, you go on to bed. I'll let myself in later."

"Thank you, Marshal. You're a very understanding gentleman."

"I'll see you in the morning."

• • •

As it happened, he saw her considerably earlier than that.

He had a few drinks in the gentlemen's lounge downstairs and lost two games out of three playing billiards with a man who looked like he would not know one end of a cue from the other, and finally went back upstairs to bed.

The room was dark, and he wished she had thought to leave a lamp burning for him. He stubbed his toe on the zinc tub that had not been there when he left the room and muttered a few curses under his breath.

He found the makeshift bed he had made for himself and sat down to pull his boots off and loosen his necktie. He removed his gunbelt and laid the double-action Colt Thunderer near his head and folded his coat to use as a pillow. That was probably as comfortable as he dared get, he decided as he stretched out on the quilt-padded floor.

"Marshal."

He had thought she was asleep.

"Yes?"

"Are you uncomfortable?" she asked.

"I can stand it."

"Would you be more comfortable up here?"

"Miss Baxter, you really ought to know that I ain't *that* much of a gentleman."

"I'm not a virgin, Marshal."

"I thought you said you were raised in a convent or some such thing."

"Yes, but I didn't say I was behind the walls *all* the time."

He thought about questioning her some more. Briefly thought about it. But, hell, he had told her himself. He wasn't so gentlemanly that he was foolish about it. She did not have to issue a second invitation.

The bed was as soft and as wide as one would expect in an expensive hotel, but it was not big enough for a woman to hide in. Longarm joined her and slipped an arm around her shoulders.

She was holding herself rigid and tight at first, but when he kissed her she relaxed, and her lips parted.

"Last chance to change your mind," he offered. So maybe sometimes he was more of a gentleman than he really wanted to be.

He could feel her shake her head in denial, then she kissed him again. It was something she was not expert at, but she was willing enough.

"Your breath tastes . . . hot," she said.

"Rye whiskey. That isn't what has the rest of me heated up, though."

"Do you really think I'm . . . attractive?"

Longarm smiled into the darkness. Now that she'd set the rules and made it clear that she wanted to play the game, she wanted to be fussed over and petted and told how terrific she was. Apparently women were the same all over, East, West, or in between.

He certainly would have thought she could tell from his physical response that she wasn't repellent to him, but obviously that was not enough. So he spent some time kissing her and telling her how beautiful and desirable she was and how badly he wanted her. Not all of it was lies.

When her breathing was ragged enough to let him know that kissing was no longer enough, he touched her breasts and rolled her nipples between his fingers. He could feel her tighten up again for a moment. Then she shuddered and gave herself to the sensations.

She was wearing a flannel sleeping gown, but it took him only a moment to pull the hem up to her waist and reach beneath it.

21

Her breasts were plump and her nipples hard. Her belly, when he trailed his fingertips lower, was as soft as a dusting of Rocky Mountain snow and as warm as a well-banked stove when that snow was lying outside the door.

She sighed and kissed him again, for the first time allowing her tongue to explore his mouth and range playfully over the hairs of his moustache.

He slid his hand between her thighs. She was wet there and very warm. Her legs parted slightly, and she raised her hips to encourage him.

"Nice," he complimented, kissing her again and enjoying the feel of her responses.

After a moment he pushed the bedcovers back and raised the hem of her gown some more so he could taste her breasts while he continued to touch and toy with her.

The movement of her hips became faster and more insistent, her breathing rapid and uneven.

After a few minutes her body stiffened and she arched her hips into the air. She moaned and thrashed her head from side to side on the down pillow.

At the end she gave one small, abrupt cry, then went limp.

"I didn't know..."

"What?"

She shook her head. "Nothing." She took his face in her hands and pulled him away from her breast and up to her mouth. She kissed him, but gently this time, slowly. "Thank you."

"My pleasure." Or soon to be.

He parted her thighs and raised himself over her to kneel between her opened legs. Her arms crept up around him and she stroked his back while he lowered himself to her.

She was still wet with her own juices, but for some reason he could not find the entry he needed.

"Guide me in," he asked of her.

One of her hands left his back and encircled him. He heard her gasp. "So *big*."

Longarm smiled. Apparently she was as willing to give a compliment as to get one.

She did as he asked, and he pressed forward into her. Even so, knowing he was there, he could feel a resistance at first.

Then, swiftly, the resistance faded and he was able to enter her fully.

She gasped again and stiffened, and he lay still on top of her to let her adjust to him there.

Only when she was relaxed did he begin to stroke slowly in and out.

She was unusually tight, her flesh a hot, gripping presence that held and titillated him, and in a much shorter time than usual he felt himself gathering toward a climax.

No longer slow and gentle, Longarm gave in to the heights of the sensation and plunged hard and deep for those last few, powerful, exhilarating strokes.

He felt her stiffen and pull back, as if he were hurting her, but it was too late to stop now, and a groan of sudden satiation was ripped from him as he came.

He felt as limp as she had just been. His release had been complete, much more so than he would have expected, and he was lightly filmed with sweat.

He leaned down to kiss her as he broke the connection between them and rolled aside.

He felt a slight, rhythmic rocking motion and touched her. She was sobbing. He touched her cheek and found tears there.

23

"Are you all right?"

"Yes, I'm just . . . happy."

"You're sure?"

"I'm sure."

She didn't sound so damn sure, but then he did not know what the trouble might be, if trouble there was. He thought it had been rather nice, actually.

"Would you mind if I have a smoke?" he asked.

He could feel her shake her head.

"Is that no, you don't mind, or, no, you'd rather I didn't smoke?"

"It's no, I don't mind if you smoke." She reached out to stop him before he could leave the bed. "Don't light the lamp, though. All right?"

"If you'd rather." Some women were funny that way, he knew. They didn't mind some hearty humping, but it was forbidden for the depleted male to see their naked bodies afterward. Seemed a strange attitude, but one Longarm wasn't going to trouble arguing with.

He felt his way to the foot of the bed, found his cheroots and matches, and carried them back to the bedside table, where there was a cuspidor handy that he could use for his ashes.

He nipped off the end of the cheroot with his teeth and chewed on it for a moment, then scraped a match aflame.

The match burned for a long time, the cheroot forgotten as Longarm's stare was directed toward the center of the bed. Eventually the flame reached Longarm's fingertips and he hastily blew it out. Even then, though, he kept looking toward where he had just seen the plump whiteness of Marianne Baxter's body and the dark vee of pubic hair beneath the hem of her gown.

24

There, streaking the insides of Marianne's thighs, was the unmistakable dark smear of blood.

The girl began to cry. "I didn't want you to know."

Longarm did not know whether to feel angry or pleased. For sure he would not have gotten into this bed with her if he had known that the damned girl was a virgin.

"You lied to me," he said finally. It sounded harsher than he had intended.

"You wouldn't have... if you had known."

Longarm grunted. She was right about that.

"I... it was my idea, you know. Cooped up in that school nearly all my life. Surrounded by nuns. I just... I think you are a nice man, Marshal. A decent man. Certainly you are attractive enough. I just... I just wanted to." She was still crying.

Nice. Decent. Attractive *enough?* Longarm was beginning to feel something like a head of beef being trotted through the stockyards back in Denver. Attractive *enough!*

"You aren't mad at me, are you?" she asked.

"I don't know yet. I'll think on it some and let you know when I decide." He found another match and this time lighted his cheroot.

"Marshal."

"Don't you think it's time you started calling me by my name, anyhow?"

The sobbing stopped, and she laughed. "Longarm."

"Yes?"

"When you do decide, well, I mean... the damage is already done. And I did think it was a nice experience. I mean... if you want to... again."

Longarm sighed. She was right, of course. What was done was done.

He finished smoking the cheroot and got back into the big bed. No point in being twice foolish.

He reached for her.

Chapter 4

Marianne watched Longarm dress in the morning, her fascination unconcealed as she observed first his facial contortions during the ritual of shaving, then the process of clothing himself, each step dictated by long habit for him but brand new and interesting to her. She seemed especially interested in the derringer soldered to his watch chain in the place of a fob and the gunbelt that he wore forward of his left hip.

When he was done she had him turn around so she could admire him from all sides.

What she saw was a tall, lean man browned by the sun and dressed mostly in brown as well. His hair and moustache were dark brown, and his tweed suit and calfskin vest and Stetson almost matched. His string tie was carefully knotted, although some time during the exertions of the night his celluloid collar had become hopelessly creased. He would have to replace it and buy some spares at the next opportunity.

"Ready for breakfast?" His tone was teasing. In her interest at watching Longarm dress, Marianne had forgotten to get dressed herself.

"I could be persuaded to stay unclothed for a little while longer," she offered.

If they had had a little more time Longarm would have been more than ready to accept that invitation. Once she had gotten into the spirit of things, so to speak, Marianne had proven to be positively eager to learn, and her education was already well progressed.

As it was, though, he had to shake his head.

"I'm perfectly willing," he said, "but the stage driver won't have as good a reason to wait. As it is, we barely have time to get a bite to eat before the coach pulls out."

Marianne pouted but began throwing on her somewhat rumpled clothing. "You said we go south from here?" she asked while she dressed.

"Uh-huh. There's two ways we could go. Monarch and Red Mountain Pass to the west or south through Poncha Pass and down to Wolf Creek. We'll go south."

"Why? I mean, I don't want to argue, but someone back in Denver told me the Red Mountain route would be quicker."

Longarm shrugged. "Quicker if things work out just right. This time of year, coming fall, you never know if there's gonna be a storm. Going Red Mountain there's more passes to cross. Too much chance of getting turned back."

Marianne, with her Eastern expectations, was obviously puzzled. "What would a storm have to do with it? Do you mean the mud could be that bad?"

Longarm laughed and stroked her cheek. "Girl, you got a lot to learn out of bed too. We aren't in Rhode Island now, and out here you can get high country snowstorms any time after, say, the third week of August. For that matter, you can get them up through maybe the second week of July. Ever been in a blizzard?"

She shook her head.

"Believe me, you don't want to be. So we'll play it safe an' go down through the San Luis Valley. The difference in the scheduled driving times is only a matter of a few hours, and this way is surer."

She acted as if she thought he might be overstating

the danger, Longarm had seen enough early fall storms to respect and fear them. And this mission was entirely too important to let it be jeopardized by a fluke in the weather.

They went down to breakfast and Longarm had the uncharitable thought that perhaps last night's unexpected invitations and sweaty tumblings had been a matter of finances more than desire, that perhaps the girl was broke and was counting on him to pay for the rest of her journey to Durango.

The suspicion was unfounded, though. She paid for her own meal, being carefully scrupulous about the division of the cost, and bought her own stage ticket as well.

The sun was still low in the eastern sky when they loaded their baggage onto the top of the much-used Studebaker mud wagon and settled into the seats they would occupy for many hours to come.

It was two full days later that the stage—with the original team and driver far behind them now—finally rolled down into the gradually flattening canyons west of Wolf Creek Pass.

The coach was running behind schedule. As Longarm had feared, they had encountered foul weather at the high elevations, and even down lower the blowing snow had been heavy in spots.

Still, the stage had already passed the worst of the road conditions before they hit weather, and the driver had brought them through it at the relatively minor expense of lost time and a strained muscle in the off leader. The big gray had been unhitched and left behind, and the stage limped into Pagosa Springs with its hot mineral baths minus one horse.

"We change teams here," the driver called back

into the coach as he pulled to a stop at the stage company station. "Road oughta be good ahead, folks, so I'm takin' 'er on through tonight. Those of you as wants to stay over can be put up at the baths, company expense since we're runnin' late, an' take the first stage down in the mornin'. Same ticket. No extry charge."

Several of the passengers in the crowded coach grumbled a desire to "let the damn line pay" for a night of comfortable lodging without the bouncing and jolting of travel. Marianne looked at Longarm and waited for his answer.

"You do what you want, of course, but I'm going on tonight."

Marianne nodded her agreement, although her expression said she would have preferred to spend the night in a hotel room. For the last hundred miles or so she had been whispering endearments into Longarm's ear that would have been shockingly personal coming from a virgin fresh out of convent school.

"Maybe in Durango?" she suggested, allowing her hand to trail lightly over his thigh. If it had still been daylight she could not have done that. As it was, with other travelers still seated close around them, she probably considered herself daring.

"Depends on the stage schedule," Longarm said. "And your daddy."

"I almost forgot," she said. "Isn't that *awful?*"

"Not very flattering for your pa, maybe, but I won't tell him if you don't."

They had time for a visit to the outhouse and a hasty—and nearly cold—meal before the stage driver called them for the rest of the trip south.

From the mineral baths on the driver was interested in maximum speed, at the expense of his passengers' comfort much of the time, and Longarm began to wonder just what the man had waiting for him in Durango. She must be something, Longarm thought, to justify that kind of speed over a bad road at night.

Still, it put him into Durango for the last leg of his journey to Gray Rock at the earliest possible time, so he had no grounds for complaint.

As it was, it was nearly two o'clock in the morning before they unloaded in the glare of lamplight outside the Durango stage station.

Longarm felt tired, his eyes gritty with dust and lack of sleep, and his limbs felt wooden. It took him a moment or two to get himself accustomed to solid ground again after the seemingly endless hours aboard the swaying coach. He was glad to be able to walk around again.

According to a schedule posted beside the stage office door it would be dawn before the next coach left for Gray Rock, so he had time enough to get Marianne established in her father's care.

"Do you have your pa's address?" he asked.

"Yes. Right here someplace." She fumbled in her handbag and after a moment's search brought out a tattered envelope that looked like it had been criss-crossing the continent for the past dozen years.

A return address, barely legible after so much handling, read: H. Baxter, Randolph Hot'l, Col. Terr. Although Colorado had been a state for some years now.

Longarm left his bags at the stage station and asked the night man for directions to the Randolph. The man gave him specific directions, ending with the inevitable, "You can't miss it."

As it turned out, the fellow had been correct. It was easy enough to find. It also turned out to be a first-class establishment.

"It looks like your pa is doing all right for himself,"

Longarm observed as he took Marianne's arm and helped her up the stairs and across the broad porch in front of the Randolph. "What does he do?"

Marianne shrugged. "I don't know, exactly. A speculator, whatever that means."

"Out here that could mean anything a man wants it to mean," Longarm said.

There was no clerk on duty in the Randolph at that hour, but the door was open and there were lamps burning in the lobby. Longarm set Marianne's bag behind the desk for safekeeping until they could get her a room—or at least determine her father's wishes on the subject—and turned the registration book around to search for H. Baxter's room number.

Apparently the Randolph served as a residential hotel for wealthy patrons, because there were few transient entries in the big ledger. It took Longarm some time to browse back through the book far enough to find Henry Baxter listed in Room 22.

"Upstairs, I think. Would you like to wait here while I go look for him?"

Marianne shook her head. She was smiling, and the excitement of the moment, the prospect of seeing her father for the first time in many years, had her practically vibrating with anxiety.

Longarm smiled at her and petted her cheek. "I don't blame you. Come on, then. Let's go see if he's in."

Marianne looked nervous and she began to babble again as Longarm led her up the stairs to the second floor. "He hasn't seen me since I was tiny *wee*," she said. "I know he won't recognize me. Oh! What if he doesn't *want* to see me?"

"Did you write to let him know you were coming?"

She shook her head. "By the time I decided, I

thought I could get here faster than a letter would. It takes a terribly long time to send a letter so far. Sometimes he would send money and it would be *months* before the letter arrived in Providence. But the sisters always knew something would be coming. Daddy never forgot to send my board money. Never. He was always good about that."

Longarm checked the room numbers at the second-floor landing and led Marianne toward the back of the hotel. Henry Baxter's room was at the far end of the hall on the left. "Here it is," he told her.

"I'm frightened."

"That's only natural, but it won't last any time at all when he sees what a fine young woman you've grown up to be." Longarm knocked loudly on the door.

He was expecting some difficulty in rousing a man out of his sleep at this late hour, but Baxter apparently was a light sleeper. He heard the man mumble something and roll out of bed before he had time to knock a second time.

"Who's there?" The voice was cold and challenging.

"Marianne." She was grinning broadly.

"Who?"

"Marianne. I'm here from Providence, Daddy."

"Oh, my *God!*" Bare feet hurried across the floor, and the door was flung wide.

Baxter was barefoot and dressed in a nightshirt. He dashed out into the hall and threw his arms around his daughter. "Marianne. Honey. What are you *doing* here?"

He looked as happy as she was, and Longarm could not help grinning.

The two hugged and held and both talked at the

same time for several minutes. Longarm stood there feeling like he was intruding, but there had been no opportunity yet for him to gracefully excuse himself and leave the two of them to their reunion.

After a time Baxter noticed the tall deputy and let go of Marianne long enough to give Longarm a questioning look.

He turned back to his daughter with a smile. "You haven't gone and brought a husband along to see your old daddy, have you?"

It was the first time Longarm had gotten a good look at Baxter since the man came into the hallway. His face had been turned away, partially obscured by Marianne's hair as they hugged.

Now Longarm had the nagging idea that he had seen Henry Baxter before.

He thought about that for a moment and concluded that they had never met.

But Longarm had seen his likeness, at the very least. He looked familiar.

"This is Mr. Long, Daddy," Marianne was saying. "Mr. Long has been a great help to me. And I couldn't have been in better hands. Mr. Long is a United States marshal, and . . ."

Baxter's face went deathly pale. His expression changed from joy to ferocious anger and fear. His lips drew back into a snarling grimace like that of a cornered predator, and without warning he grabbed Marianne's shoulders and threw the girl against Longarm, tangling the two of them there in the hallway while Baxter bolted back into his room.

"Damn it!"

Marianne's squeal of shocked surprise went unheard by either man as Longarm disengaged himself from her and stepped into the doorway with the big Colt in his fist.

"Don't, Baxter. *Don't!*"

The man had reached the nightstand beside his bed. He grabbed up a revolver and, dropping into a crouch, spun to face the door.

"Please don't," Longarm shouted.

But Henry Baxter was not listening. His thumb fumbled for the hammer of the single-action Smith and Wesson .44 Russian.

Longarm had no choice. The Colt bellowed, spitting flame and smoke into the hotel room. The sound of the gunshot in such close confinement was deafening, and the burnt powder stank of acid fumes in such close quarters.

The .45 caliber slug took Baxter high in the shoulder and spun him rudely to the side.

"Drop it, Baxter. I don't want to take you this way," Longarm shouted.

Either the man did not believe him or did not hear after the first crash of Longarm's Colt, but for whatever reason he did not heed Longarm's repeated pleas for him to surrender.

"Think about Marianne, man. Drop the gun. Now!"

Baxter regained his balance and again tried to level his gun at the big deputy.

Hating to do it but knowing that he was given no choice, Longarm triggered the Colt again.

Marianne Baxter's father died with a bullet through his heart.

Sick with the anger of frustration, Longarm hurried to make sure there was no more threat from the fallen Baxter, then ran back out into the hall.

Marianne was crumpled on the floor, and for one awful instant Longarm thought she might have been struck by a stray bullet. But Baxter had not fired. The girl had fainted.

Longarm holstered his Colt and bent over her. He

could hear footsteps pounding on the stairs as someone ran to see what had happened—a common but foolish response when guns were being fired.

Longarm kept shaking his head in denial, but there was no denying the ugly truth. Without ever meaning to harm her, in the past few days he had taken from this girl everything she possessed. And now there was no changing it. None of it could ever be returned to her.

He could not even remember what name Baxter had been using on the wanted poster Longarm had seen of him or what crimes the man had been wanted for. That seemed somehow insulting to the dead man and to his unfortunate daughter.

Longarm turned to face the hotel keeper and the guests who were pouring out into the hallway now. He hoped they had some efficient people providing local law here. He wanted to get the hell out of Durango the very first second that was possible. He wanted out of here. Now. Before Marianne woke up and looked at him with the accusation that would have to be in her eyes.

He really did not want to have to face that.

Chapter 5

Gray Rock was aptly named. It was set at the edge of the foothills that rose like ever higher waves, frozen in time, from the flat, dry desert country to the south and west toward the high, craggy San Juan mountain range to the northeast.

The San Juans were sprinkled mottled white with snow now. Later in the season, possibly within a matter of weeks, they would be solidly capped with high snowfields where the snow depths would be measured in yards, not inches, until next summer.

Nearer, to the west of the San Juans, the land gradually descended in hills and ridges until the stark, red rock and caliche of the canyon-cut flatlands were reached. From here the desert marched off to the south for hundreds of miles, reaching far down into Mexico and becoming ever drier and ever harsher as it went.

Gray Rock was situated at the base of a massive rock formation that was the last outpost of the San Juans, a solid, jutting massif of gray granite set at the edge of the red sandstone formations of the desert.

The distinctive color was startling against the red and yellow hues of the land beyond it, and the name of the town would have been a natural description before veins of gold-bearing ore were discovered hidden within the granite.

The town itself was sprawling and haphazardly assembled. Streets were laid out by usage rather than design, and there were more of them than Longarm would have expected.

The population too at first glance seemed more than he had expected.

There were, of course, miners, who would work underground at the big mine he could see built against the gray dome of granite on the north side of the town. From the main street he could easily see the shaft hoists and tailings dump of the mine spilling down the side of the gray hill.

More than the miners, though, there were stockmen on the streets, and from the windows of the stage he had seen several small farms along the creek that wound past the south edge of the town.

Probably, he thought, the cattlemen would have been here first. Then the miners when the gold was discovered. Last the farmers, taking the opportunity presented to irrigate small fields from the stream of mountain runoff and sell their produce to both miners and stockmen. He wondered idly if the stockmen and the farmers would be able to sustain the life of a town here when the mine eventually petered out. And die the mine must when the supply of available gold from its veins was someday exhausted.

Longarm looked closely as the stage rolled to a stop, but he could see no Indians anywhere on the streets of the town.

Not a good sign, he realized. Wherever there were stores, anywhere within a hundred miles of any Indian agency, there should certainly be Indian customers for the wares of those stores.

And the Utes had adapted to white tastes, if not as yet to white styles of living, much more than nearly any other of the Western tribes. Not as much, say, as the Indian Territory's Five Civilized Tribes. But far earlier and far easier than the rowdy Arapaho and Cheyenne and Comanche.

38

He did not like to see their absence now from the streets of Gray Rock.

But at least it looked as if there were not yet any open hostilities. Men and women walked comfortably in the streets, and not all of the men were armed here.

There was still time, he hoped.

He claimed his luggage from the roof rack of the Studebaker and headed immediately toward a sign he could see down the street indicating the town marshal's office and jail.

The only thing he knew about the marshal here was that Billy Vail said the man sent telegrams as if he had to pay for every word of the message out of his own pocket. The marshal's name, again according to Billy, was J. Briscoe.

Like most of the buildings in Gray Rock, the marshal's office was made of adobe brick plastered over with lime. Thin vigas, little more than saplings when they had been cut and hauled, protruded beyond the walls at ceiling height. Wood would be scarce here and difficult to obtain, but the adobe could be produced from materials already at hand. As always, though, the mud-brick buildings set onto dry country gave the whole town a depressing sameness of form and color. Longarm much preferred the mountains and the greener plains he had so recently left.

Longarm entered the open doorway of the town marshal's office and stopped short. He quickly swept his hat off and nodded.

"I'm looking for Marshal Briscoe, ma'am."

The only person in the place was a woman. She was tall and not quite yet to middle age. She wore a dark blue velveteen gown with a panel of white ruffles high around her throat and a matching blue hat over a tight-pinned mass of dark hair that was beginning to be sprinkled with gray. A handbag and, oddly, a riding crop were laid on the desk where she was seated. She did not look as if she was dressed for riding. Her dress, very conservative, showed nothing of her figure.

"Yes?" she said.

Longarm looked around the room. There was no one there, not even any prisoners in the two cells at the back of the one-room structure.

"Could I set my things down here?"

"Of course."

He placed his carpetbag and saddle in a corner and tried his queston again. "I'm looking for the town marshal, ma'am."

She gave him a somewhat suspicious looking-over and said, "I suppose you are going to tell the marshal that you can recover the missing money? For a percentage, of course. Tell me, am I supposed to appreciate your honesty since you are coming here first instead of just going out and taking it for yourself? Is that what I am supposed to think?"

Longarm smiled at her. "I think I see the problem, ma'am. And unfortunately I *am* going to tell you that I'm here to recover the money. Although personally, if it wasn't for the idiots who've obviously been coming in here with their palms itchy from greed, well, I'd be happier just to leave both the money and the old chief where they are. The plain fact is, though, some fool is going to dig it up. And I reckon I'm the fool that's appointed."

He pulled out his wallet and flipped it open for her to see. "Now, ma'am, if you could tell me where to find Marshal Briscoe . . . ?"

The woman's reaction was not exactly what he might have expected. She sat back in her chair and closed her eyes. "Thank God," she said. "Thank God,

Marshal, that you've come."

"Ma'am?"

She opened her eyes and sat upright again. Now that he looked closer, Longarm could see that this woman had been under a considerable amount of strain recently. She looked tired and probably would have been quite attractive without the haunted look in her eyes and the dark circles of fatigue beneath them.

She stood and extended a hand toward him. Not knowing what else to do, Longam gently shook with her.

"I am Jean Briscoe, Marshal Long. And I am the town marshal of Gray Rock."

"Ma'am?"

Marshal Jean Briscoe stirred a second spoonful of sugar into her tea and nibbled at the edge of a cookie. They were seated at a corner table in the restaurant of the only hotel in Gray Rock. The lady marshal was having a mid-afternoon snack while Longarm attempted to make up for the meals he had lost in his hurry to get here.

"What it is, Deputy, is an honorary sort of thing. At least that was what was intended. My late husband was one of the early settlers in this part of the country. He ran cattle here long before gold was discovered. He was well known and well liked, both by the old-timers and by the mining people. Last year he had a terrible fall from a rank horse. He couldn't ride any longer and had to sell the ranch and all of our cattle. The townspeople offered him the job of marshal here. It wasn't an unreasonable offer. There has never been a problem with crime here, and Burton was more than capable of handling the few duties." She sighed and took a sip of her tea.

"Last month Burton died. The doctors said his lungs

filled with fluid, probably as a result of that fall, until they simply did not work any longer. Burton had been a very well-liked man. He got along with everyone. Just everyone. When he died..." She shrugged. "As a courtesy to his memory more than anything else, they asked me to fill his place until an election could be held. I... suppose it has been no secret that I was not left... well off. The salary is small, but frankly I can use it. Like I say, the offer was a courtesy to Burton's memory and a gesture to me as well, I suppose. I thought it kind of them. I still do. Certainly none of us envisioned anything like this happening in Gray Rock. It... just never occurred to us. I suppose it should have."

Longarm politely refrained from shaking his head. Local law was often fouled by politics. Here it seemed that kindness and good will had gotten in the way instead.

"Have you conducted an investigation?" he asked.

Jean Briscoe looked embarrassed. "Probably not what *you* would call an investigation."

"What did you do, Mrs. Briscoe? I mean, Marshal."

She almost smiled. "Mrs. Briscoe suits me better than this silly title, I assure you."

"As you wish, ma'am."

"All I've done is talk, basically. I mean, when that gang went riding out of here there were a good many men in pursuit of them already. I hadn't time to deputize a posse. To tell you the truth, I wouldn't have known what to say if I did have more time. So I left that to them and telegraphed ahead for assistance from the Ute police. They have their own police force, you know, with Indian officers."

"Yes, ma'am, I know about that."

"Of course you would. Forgive me for my ignorance, please. I keep forgetting that the Ute officers operate under federal authority, just as you do."

"If you know that, Mrs. Briscoe, you have a better understanding of the situation than most," Longarm told her.

"Thank you. Anyway, I went first to the telegraph office, then to the bank. I found Walker Hardifer—he was president of the bank—shot to death beside the open vault door. His teller, Jim MacGinnis, was lying beside a desk approximately ten feet from the vault. Both men were dead. Sam Cane, Walker's vice president, was on the floor beside Walker's body. Sam's scalp was bloody. There was more blood from his wounds, in fact, than from the two deaths. He had been beaten rather severely with the barrel of a revolver. The injuries required a number of stitches. He says he does not remember if any of the robbers shot at him, but I think it entirely possible that they thought he was already dead or dying when they left.

"I called a doctor to look after Sam's wounds, of course. It was impossible to determine how much money was stolen until Sam was able to assist me, so while the doctor was working on Sam I closed and relocked the vault. The vault is one of those with a clockwork mechanism that only allows it to be opened at a pre-determined time. The Gray Rock Bank vault is set to open daily at 3:10 P.M. to handle the day's deposits. A smaller amount of cash is kept in a combination safe, for daily business, you understand, and it is understood that major withdrawals have to be made after notice of at least a full business day."

"That's common knowledge in town?" Longarm asked.

"Yes. Certainly among the business people who

43

would have occasion to make large withdrawals. I doubt that many individual depositors would know of the policy."

Longarm nodded and waited for the woman to go on.

"As it happened, there was a large sum of cash in the time vault on the day of the robbery. The Halleluia payroll was in there."

"The Halleluia?"

"I'm sorry. Of course you would not know. The Halleluia is the name of the mine you may have noticed on the hillside."

Longarm nodded again. "You relocked the vault. I assume it was empty at the time."

"Yes. I checked the boxes first, then closed the vault and made sure the lock had caught. I also checked the smaller safe. It was standing open, ready to receive the overnight cash. It was empty also, but the cash drawers at the two windows had not been disturbed. They contained what I assume was a normal amount of working cash. Apparently the robbers concentrated first on the vault containing the payroll and did not have time to take the lesser amount from the cash drawers."

"Have you found out how much was taken?"

"Oh, yes. Sam felt well enough the next day to go over the books. The amount was slightly in excess of eighty thousand dollars. I have the exact figure written down in Bur . . . in my office."

Longarm whistled. That was a hell of a haul for a bunch of inept thieves. "There were how many in the gang?" he asked.

"Eight."

Ten thousand dollars per man, and a shade more. A mine worker here probably got two dollars a day, a cowhand somewhat less than that. Ten thousand dollars would keep a man in thick gravy for an awfully long time.

"What about the dead gang members?" Longarm asked.

"I had them buried, of course."

"No, ma'am, I mean, what about their identities? Did you know any of them? Were any of them local boys?"

Mrs. Briscoe shook her head. "None. I'm sure of that. Why do you ask?"

"To tell you the truth, ma'am, I'm hoping that the missing money is not in that grave out at the agency. I was thinking maybe if they were local they'd have had somebody friendly they could have passed the money to on their way out of town. You know. To hold it for them till they got away. Something like that."

"I'm sorry to disappoint you, Deputy, but they were in sight the entire way out of town, from the moment they left the bank door. The posse was only minutes behind them and reported seeing no one in the chase out to the agency." She sighed. "I really should have thought of that, shouldn't I? Thank goodness there's a professional here now." She gave him a look of real gratitude.

"Ma'am, you keep talking about how this job is a courtesy and all that, but let me tell you something true. I've known some mighty rugged he-coons, men who've been wearing badges for twenty years and more, who couldn't have given me as thorough or as good a report as you just did. Or who couldn't have handled the crime scene half as good. You did just fine, Marshal Briscoe. Just fine indeed."

The woman looked as though she wanted to be

45

pleased by the compliment but was afraid to believe him.

"No, ma'am," he added, "there's a lot more to crime investigation than shooting fast or riding hard. I'd say you're doing good."

"Thank you."

He thought he saw a faint hint of a blush on her cheeks. And, what the hell, he had only told her the truth.

Longarm's meal arrived, and he dug gratefully into the tallow-fried steak and fried potatoes. As soon as possible, although he was not looking forward to it, he was going to have to hire a horse and ride out to the Los Pinos Agency.

The damned exhumation order was in his coat pocket, and he was as conscious of the thing as if it had been a white-hot branding iron instead of a simple piece of paper.

Chapter 6

Longarm hunkered down on his heels beside the open fire pit and accepted the offer of a charred piece of meat that might have had any origin—he hoped it was venison, but would not have been amazed if it was dog instead—and a cup of fiery trade whiskey. The liquor was, of course, entirely illegal. He took a swallow of the miserable stuff and grinned his appreciation. A small test applied by his hosts, he thought, both by way of the awful whiskey itself and its illegality. Under the circumstances, he thought it best to make no mention of the breach of federal law. Better by far to make it clear in this small way that he had not come here intending to be hard-nosed and angry.

He could not help noticing that there were a great many dark eyes watching his every move as he swallowed off the rest of the rank liquor and asked for a refill. So far so good. He took a bite of the meat, nodded, and managed a complimentary belch. The amenities were in order.

All around the fire pit he could see the homes of the agency Utes. The Utes here, adapting to white ways, had not abandoned their skin lodges, but at home at the agency they kept them packed away. Now they were living in more or less permanent structures that were about midway between jacales and cabins.

There were several positively white-looking small houses on the fringes of the area, and far off to one side was a rather nice-looking frame house, white-painted and pretty, with a white picket fence surrounding it. Longarm probably would have assumed that it was the agency superintendent's home if he had not already been told about the place. It was the house the government had built for Ouray as part of the settlement that brought the Utes back in from the warpath last year.

For the purposes of this conference, though, the men were gathered around an open council fire. So far Longarm had no idea which of them, if any, was in charge now that Ouray was dead and the real leadership of the tribe was in doubt.

The Indians who were hunkered around the fire in a circle with him would not have met the expectations of an Easterner's idea of what an Indian should be. There was not a breechclout nor a feather in sight, and not a single face was daubed with anything more outrageous or uncivilized than a stray smudge of dirt here and there. And Longarm probably had that much added color on his own face after four hours in the saddle reaching the place.

Most of the men wore woolen trousers and cotton shirts. Most wore hats, castoff military issue and civilian styles alike. One of the dark-complected men facing him across the fire wore a business suit—several seasons past due for a cleaning, but a well-made suit nonetheless—and a derby hat.

What made them look different from a group of grubby miners was the dark copper of their skins, the necklaces which festooned their chests, and the comfortable moccasins they wore instead of boots.

"Good," Longarm said. He finished the meat and tossed the bone—suspiciously small for anything that might have grown on a deer—into the fire.

He took a fistful of cheroots from his coat pocket

and passed them around to the men. He had stocked up on cheroots before he left Gray Rock that morning. There were, he noticed, no women anywhere in sight.

When he had his own smoke fired to his satisfaction, Longarm rocked back onto his heels and waited. There was no sense in being pushy so early. It would only make the Utes more uneasy than they already were.

And they were definitely uneasy. Not a single one of them said or did anything to indicate that, but the absence of the women from the area said it well enough for them.

They were edgy. They did not know just how high-handed and ugly this emissary from the government was going to be. The wrong move now, any hint of arrogance or belligerence, could spook the whole crowd.

Longarm waited and smoked his cigar patiently.

"You are the one called Long Arm," the man in the derby said eventually.

"I am," Longarm agreed. He took another puff on the cheroot. "I do not remember you." He wondered how many of these men spoke English. Probably all of them, although some might not be willing to admit it. Old Ouray had taught himself both English and Spanish so he could dicker to best advantage for his people regardless of the circumstances. And the Utes had been in pretty much constant contact with the whites for something like fifty years now, most of that time peacefully. Longarm took another pull at the cheroot and made a show of examining its coal; he was in no hurry.

The man in the derby ignored the implied question and said, "You wear your guns. Are you not among friends?"

Longarm nodded. "I am among friends. Do friends have anything to fear from a friend's gun?" If they thought they could get him to leave his guns on the hired horse, they were wrong. That would be a show of weakness, not trust.

The man in the derby ignored that question and returned to the first one. "I am John Badger."

Longarm grunted and nodded. The name was obviously how the man was known to the whites; it might or might not have had any bearing on his real name. If Longarm had ever heard of him before it must have been under his true name, but John Badger would do for the time being. And since Badger was doing the talking, it followed that he must be one of the Utes in contention for leadership now that Ouray was out of the picture.

"Do I know you, John Badger?"

"I have seen you at the council. I know the man called Long Arm."

Longarm grunted again and smoked some more.

"The man called Long Arm has been trusted," Badger said after a while. "Would he break that trust now?"

"No." Longarm sat hunkered on his heels. He finished the cheroot and tossed the butt into the fire.

"Yet you come here to bring us harm," Badger said.

Kind of pushy and blunt of him for an Indian, Longarm thought. He had not expected to get to the point so soon. "I come here to preserve the peace, not to break it."

"The place of burial is sacred."

"Ouray was a Methodist," Longarm said. "Methodists don't follow the same path as the old ways."

That excuse—reasoning?— was not thrown out

50

casually. He had given the subject a lot of thought over the past few days. And that right there was the only argument he could come up with that might help them all get out of this without a war. If he could convince them that an exhumation was all right for a Methodist even though it was sacrilege for a Ute, maybe, just maybe...

Badger chewed on that for some time while he finished the cheroot Longarm had given him. Longarm's hopes began to rise. At least there was no immediate rejection of his reasoning.

"The Arrow—" for some reason Badger Anglicized the dead chief's name now—"was Ute first."

Longarm gave it some time before he answered. To speak at once would have implied that he did not care enough about the Indian's words to consider them. "The Arrow was a Methodist last."

At least five minutes of total silence went by, long enough that one of the younger men left the circle and returned with wood to feed the fire. Longarm did not like to see that the man had done the chore himself instead of calling for a woman to bring the wood.

"We are Ute," Badger grunted. His tone of voice was mighty firm, Longarm thought.

Longarm waited a while and said, "You are Ute."

Again there was a long silence. "You will wait. Stay here tonight. We will talk. Tomorrow we will talk again with the man called Long Arm."

"I could come back tomorrow." The prospect of sleeping with fleas was not an inviting one.

Badger shook his head. "Snow tonight. Better you stay."

Longarm could not help raising his eyes to look at the sky to the west and then to the south, the two directions weather was likely to come from. Nowhere could he see a cloud of any sort, much less a threatening dark cloud. And a storm? Damned unlikely. Down here they had not even had any of the snow he and the girl had encountered back in the San Juans. The ground and the grass, what there was of it, was brown and dry.

Still, Badger was making a point of him staying. They might be afraid that if he left he would bring troops with him when he returned. Or some other thing, a superstition or omen, might be at work here, something no white man could ever hope to understand.

If they wanted him to stay, Longarm concluded, stay he would.

He nodded his acceptance of the request.

"Better you give us your guns," Badger said, testing once again for weakness now that he had gotten a concession from the man he called Long Arm.

"No." No fuss or argument, just a simple refusal.

Badger nodded. He had learned what he wanted to know. "Tonight we will eat together. Then we will talk. Tomorrow we talk again to Long Arm."

Longarm nodded.

Badger's eyes twinkled for a moment. "Short Leg will show you to your place for the night."

Longarm appreciated John Badger's play on words but was careful not to smile. He played it straight, which probably added to the old boy's amusement, letting him think he had slipped a joke past the white government man.

Badger turned and waved his arm, and a young woman with a twisted leg came out of one of the houses to join them and lead Longarm away.

Interesting, Longarm thought, that they had had this set up ahead of time. They had to have, because the house was too far away from the fire for the woman to have overheard, yet a wave of Badger's hand was enough instruction for her to know what was required.

Longarm stood and left the fire without a backward glance.

Come to think of it, he realized, they not only had this part worked out, they had known it would be the man they called Long Arm who would be coming to their council.

He wondered what else they might know. And whether they would be willing to share with him the things he should know about all of this.

Chapter 7

Supper was not exactly a feast. A good many of the Utes were acting much too restrained for that, probably as a result of the uncertainties that lay between them and any white man right now. But it was festive enough, considering.

The women were in evidence now and the fires burning high. The children were also showing themselves, flitting along the edges of the gathering of grown folk. The boys in the eight-to-ten age range somehow arrived at a game that had to do with sneaking up on the white visitor and counting coup on him with a grass stem. Longarm let them get away with it, pretending not to notice them until he felt the soft touch of the grass on his arm. Then, each time, he expressed surprise. The children's elders noticed his deception, and while they said nothing to him about it, he thought they approved.

The meal was army-issue beef, army-issue beans rather badly undercooked, and army-issue coffee. At least there seemed to be enough of it, Longarm noticed.

Off to one side a number of the men gathered around a large crock of homemade trade whiskey. None of them got drunk, though, and Longarm also pretended not to notice this.

When the meal was over, the women and children disappeared again. Longarm took that as his cue to head for the mud-and-stick jacal which had been given to him for the night. Throughout the entire evening, no one had spoken a word to him about anything more important than whether he wanted a second helping of beef.

He went back to the jacal and dropped the blanket that served as a door. There was already a crockery lamp burning in one corner of the place. The lamp and a pile of blankets on the floor to serve as a bed were the only furnishings in the hut.

He was not alone.

"Hello."

Short Leg sat up, blinking. She must have dozed while she was waiting for him. She smiled at him but did not speak. When she sat up the blanket that had been over her fell to her waist. She was naked except for a pair of bone and silver necklaces and a layer of grease.

"Are you . . . ?" He did not know how he ought to finish the question. Not in so many words. Besides, it was painfully obvious what her intention was. She was naked and in his bed. Apparently the Utes were being more hospitable than he expected or wanted. He had, after all, had a chance to get a whiff of Short Leg earlier in the afternoon. He had smelled buffalo not half as ripe.

The woman—she was not young enough to be called a girl by any wild stretch of the imagination—smiled at him again and patted the bed beside her ample bottom.

Longarm smiled back at her. Somehow.

Now that he had reason to look at her closely, he did so. What he saw was not a lot more encouraging than the odor had been. She was dumpy, thick-bodied and flabby-breasted. She had a round face that he could not help likening to a mud-daubed spade . . . at least that flat and rounded. And those were her good points. When she smiled he could see that she was missing several teeth.

Longarm leaned back against the wall of the jacal. He would not really have minded a hell of a lot if the whole shaky structure had come tumbling down from his weight leaning against it. At least then he would have had an excuse to get out of this.

But, damn it, if he refused the Ute hospitality, would the nation decide they had been insulted?

As far as he knew that might be the only excuse they needed to go ahead and start a war that seemed inevitable to them anyway. They just might take that as an excuse so they could get the first licks in if there was going to be fighting anyhow.

The thought was distressing, but only marginally more so than the idea of bedding this homely squaw.

The damn Utes, it seemed, had Long Arm by the short hairs.

The woman smiled at him again and stood up. A fuller view of her sagging, filthy flesh did not improve her any. She came over to his side and stood there expectantly.

It was all Longarm could do to keep from wrinkling his nose. He smiled at her.

Beyond the blanket-curtain that covered the door, Longarm's always-active ears caught a hint of sound that should not have been there.

He held a finger up to his lips, motioning Short Leg to silence, and listened more closely.

Someone was out there, slipping up on the door of the jacal the way the children had crept up behind him at supper. But these careful footfalls were heavier. It would be a grown man who was out there. Probably more than one or he would not have had any chance to hear them at all.

Were they waiting to jump him, then, as soon as he had delivered the insult?

The Colt was there, ready if he needed it. But it would be a certain declaration of war if he used it, regardless of provocation. Suspicions damn sure would never be accepted as a reasonable explanation.

He chuckled. If that was what happened, hell, he wouldn't have to worry about explaining anything to anyone afterward. There was no way in the world he could shoot his way clear of a whole agency full of stirred-up Utes.

Then another thought struck him.

This time he did not chuckle. This time he threw his head back and laughed outright.

"I love a man with a sense of humor, John Badger," Longarm said in a normal tone of voice.

From a distance not more than two feet away from his head but on the other side of the blanket he heard a series of low grunts that might well have been contained laughter.

Longarm grinned. So this whole thing had been another of Badger's little tests, with a joke thrown in for the fun of it.

John Badger stepped inside the jacal. "How did Long Arm know?"

Longarm grinned at him. "I'll admit you had me scared at first. But I've been around the Ute long enough to know that you are a clean people. You bathe even in the winter when the whites do not. No woman of your people would come to a guest as this one did."

This was partially true. Longarm was not about to

tell the man that he had heard him sneaking around outside. John Badger might not have appreciated that.

Badger's face contorted like he had something sour in his mouth, and he let out another string of those low grunts that seemed to be his way of laughing. "Long Arm is clever." He paused a fraction of a second and added, "For a white."

"John Badger is a good man." Pause. "For a Ute."

There was only the smallest of changes at the corner of John Badger's eyes, a hint of a twinkle in the dark pupils.

Badger said something to the girl that was much too fast for Longarm to catch any of its meaning.

Short Leg grinned happily and with a squeal of pleasure dashed out past the two men.

"Going to take a bath, I expect?" Longarm asked.

John Badger nodded. "My sister. I had to threaten to beat her to make her stay so for this long." Abruptly he said, "I go now."

The derby-wearing Indian turned and left the jacal. Longarm still had not been able to peg an age to the man, although something at the far end of the middle years might have been right.

Longarm, grinning, let the blanket drop back in place across the doorway, then went to the bed that had been prepared for him.

He stripped to his balbriggans and laid his holstered Colt beside his head. A small bag of something, coarse sand possibly or grains of rice, had been provided as a pillow. He plumped it into as acceptable a shape as possible and blew out the oil lamp with its floating wick of twisted wool thread.

"Good night, John Badger." That was a shot, as well as a voice, in the dark. This time he hadn't heard or sensed a damn thing outside the hut. But if someone was there, it would impress them. If not, there was no harm done because no one would ever know.

Smiling into the darkness, Longarm closed his eyes and went to sleep. Somewhere beyond the thin walls of the jacal he could hear the crackling of a huge fire and a low murmur of voices speaking a language he did not understand. No sense in worrying about it now. He would know soon enough what they decided.

Longarm came awake instantly. He sat up, and his hand found the Colt exactly where it was supposed to be.

The movement of the blanket falling from his shoulders must have been heard because instantly there was a gentle, cautioning voice from the shadows. A woman's voice.

"Short Leg?"

He sniffed, but even when the woman reached his side he could smell nothing but clean woman-flesh from bathing. It could have been Short Leg, or any other female of any race at all. He just could not tell.

He heard a rustle of cloth and then felt the warmth of naked flesh at his side as the woman joined him on the bed.

A little hospitality after all. The genuine article this time.

Longarm draped an arm around her waist. Her body was thick, like Short Leg's, but then so were ninety percent of the Ute women he had seen that evening.

The woman—girl? He just did not know—said something to him in her own language. It sounded like it was meant to be reassuring, so Longarm took it that way.

"Whatever you say, honey."

The woman lay down beside him and spread herself. She reached for him in the darkness, finding and fondling his crotch.

Longarm's male reaction to her gentle touch was automatic. He came to attention, and the woman giggled her pleasure and stroked him lightly with her fingertips.

He got the impression that she was enjoying the size of him. She kept touching him and caressing him, alternately toying with him that way and hefting the weight of his balls in her palm.

She whispered something to him, repeating it several times, but Longarm had not the faintest idea what she was saying.

Eventually she wanted more from her toy than being able to touch it.

Gently but insistently she tugged him over and onto her. Without having to be asked she greedily guided his way, arching her hips to receive him and sighing when he was socketed deep inside her.

He began to move, to pump and stroke softly in and out, but after only a moment of that the woman stopped him with a touch and a light application of pressure to his rump. She said something again. When Longarm tried to stroke again she stopped him once more and repeated the phrase she had just used.

"All right, if you have somethin' else in mind."

He held himself stiff, poised over her but still within her.

The woman moved beneath him. At first he thought she was only shifting position. Then he realized that she was raising her hips, impaling herself on his shaft while he remained motionless just above her.

She whispered something and moved again, with more assurance this time, setting the rhythms and performing the work while Longarm did nothing but remain still and experience the sensations of her wet, gently gripping flesh around him.

She pumped up and down, stroking deeper and slightly faster now.

Damned if this didn't feel good, Longarm thought. Really good.

He told her so, but if she understood English she was not willing to admit that to him.

Apparently she was as ready as he was now. He could hear a speeding up in her breathing, and she began to pump faster.

Once Longarm tried to join her, but once again she stopped him, this time with a solid rap on his butt to make him remain motionless while she finished the job at hand.

She was pumping vigorously now, and her breath was definitely ragged.

Longarm could feel his own response building.

He held himself tight against the climbing spill, willing himself not to come. Not yet. Not quite . . .

The women yelped and writhed beneath him as she achieved her own demanding satisfaction, and that was enough to dump Longarm over the last edge of control.

He plunged forward, hard and fast, bucking and thrusting in the last throes of feeling now.

When he was done he felt limp and thoroughly drained, as if she had taken the strength from him as well as his seed.

Gently the Ute woman rolled him onto his back. She found a cloth in the darkness, her own dress probably, and used it to sponge off his sweaty chest and belly.

"Thanks," Longarm muttered.

She said something. This time he did not particularly care what it was. Nor did she seem to expect any answer.

Longarm closed his eyes. When he opened them again there was a faint shading of coming daylight at the edges of the blanket, and the woman was gone. He was alone on the bed. He rolled over and reached for a cheroot and match. He might never know who she had been. But there was always that old saying to fall back on, the one about gift horses.

He chuckled. Not a bad gift John Badger had sent him.

Chapter 8

John Badger shaved tobacco from a dark, twisted plug into the palm of his hand. Then, with a slow deliberation that approached ceremony, he filled and lighted the pipe.

The pipe itself looked old and important. The bowl was carved from red stone, the stem a two-foot length of willow bark with the wood and pith removed. Bowl and stem alike were hung with tufts of curly, downy feathers. Longarm wondered if the feathers had a significance of their own or if they were only for decoration. This did not seem like the time to ask.

Badger closed his eyes while he puffed the pipe alight, then blew smoke in the four directions and passed the pipe to an elderly Ute who looked more like what an Indian was expected to look like. A shaman perhaps, the old man wore leather clothes almost as old as he was, liberally ornamented with intricate quill work. He too blew smoke in the four directions but also to the sky and to the earth. Then the pipe passed around to all the members of the circle, including the white guest from the federal government.

Longarm took his puff in turn. The long, hollow stem gave the smoke ample time to cool as it passed from bowl to mouth. It was a good smoke, quite apart from the ceremony of it all.

All of the men except John Badger and the old shaman had merely puffed at the pipe and passed it on. On impulse, Longarm took a deep pull on the stem and blew out short, slow puffs in each of the four directions, north, south, east, and west, then to the sky and the earth as well. He was not sure, but he thought he saw approval in John Badger's eyes. He passed the pipe on around the circle.

When the pipe returned to Badger he gave it reverently to the old man, who used a carved bone tool to clean out the coal and ash, then wrapped the ceremonial device in an elaborately decorated piece of deerskin and placed both into a deep, narrow parfleche that had obviously been made for that purpose. He laid the covered and protected pipe aside, and John Badger cleared his throat.

Longarm waited patiently for Badger to gather his thoughts.

"It would be better for the bones of the Arrow to remain undisturbed," John Badger said in a casual tone of voice.

Longarm could have responded immediately, but that would have been impolite. It would have implied that he was not giving due consideration to what Badger said. So he sat for a while in silence.

In theory, he was supposed to be considering that statement carefully. Actually, he was hoping that Badger would say something more. Hell, he thought, the men had sat up half the night talking about this. And all Badger had said so far was the perfectly obvious. Hell, yes, it would be better if Ouray's grave was not disturbed. But in point of fact, as long as one resident of Gray Rock believed the missing fortune might be buried there, that grave was damn sure going to be dug up. If not immediately, then on some dark night in the future. The point here was how to avoid that event turning into a war between the Utes and every white man, woman, and child in Colorado and the surrounding states and territories.

Badger said nothing more, so eventually Longarm equivocated with a simple, "This is true."

Badger gave him the courtesy of a lengthy think-it-over period. Longarm might have wished for a little less courtesy from the Utes at this gathering. He felt a mighty urge to scratch his crotch and spend the time hoping he had not picked up some tiny livestock down there during the past night.

"I will show you the inside of our hearts," Badger said finally.

Longarm nodded. Good. Maybe now they were going to get down to it.

"There are those among us who loved the Arrow and looked to him as our leader, much as your people did but in not the same way."

He paused, and after a moment Longarm nodded again. It was no surprise to him that the official concept of chief was a hell of a far cry from the Indian notion of it. To a white man, a chief was supposed to be a boss, something on the order of a military officer who had charge of a unit of enlisted men. But to an Indian, a chief was someone they mostly respected and *might* choose to follow... if they liked whatever it was he was suggesting. But he damn sure had no authority to *order* them to do anything. The difference between those two concepts was vast, and it had led to serious misunderstandings between the two races ever since the two came in contact with one another. When a chief signed a treaty, the whites figured that it was binding on an entire tribe or nation. But the Indians figured it binding only on the fellow who put his mark to the piece of paper, not the rest of the crowd. Ouray had been a strong leader of the

65

Utes, but not at all in the way the bureaucrats in Washington thought of him.

"This I understand," Longarm said.

Badger nodded. "Good." He paused again. "There are some among us who cared nothing for the Arrow. But to them also the place of burial is sacred. It must not be disturbed." Badger paused and scratched himself. Longarm felt a great sense of relief knowing it would not be a breach of etiquette to scratch his own itches. He put his nails to work. Damn, that felt better.

"It is true," Badger went on, "that some of our people would wish for a chance to go out once again with paint and carbines and make the land run red with the blood of our enemies."

Preventing that from happening had probably been what Ouray had been best at. Now, it seemed, that job was up to John Badger. And Custis Long.

"They are not happy," Badger was saying, "that the White River country was taken from us. They do not like Los Pinos. They wish to return to White River and to the place your people call the South Park."

No big surprise there. The White River Agency had been closed last year after the Meeker massacre and the outbreak that followed it. South Park had been effectively denied to them ever since gold was discovered there twenty or so years earlier. Either was a better country than this one.

"If your people bring the bones of the Arrow back to the world of sun and grass," Badger said, "there must surely be war between us. And I would have to take up my gun and kill the man called Long Arm." Badger's face was blank of expression. He looked Longarm in the eyes while he waited for the white man to answer.

Longarm waited a while and said, trying to flower

66

it up some, "John Badger could have been my brother if my skin was dark or if his was light. But if there is war between us I will have to take up my gun and kill John Badger. This I would rather not do."

No long pause this time. Badger's face showed nothing, but apparently they were getting to the heart of it now. "Do not dig in the final place of the Arrow."

"If I do not," Longarm said, "if you do not help me so that together white and Ute can solve this problem, then surely some white man with greed in his heart and no love for the Ute will come and dig and do this thing that will cause a war between us."

Badger's face remained impassive, as expressionless as carved stone. Or a death mask. "There is no need to dig. The act would be insult alone. There is no gold buried with the Arrow."

"Your customs do not call for the burial of riches with your dead, no, but . . ."

John Badger's expression still showed nothing, but the man committed the astounding impropriety of holding up a hand to halt Longarm in mid-sentence. "I know of the theft. It was our police and those of our Nadene cousins who emptied their blood into the ground. I say to you, there is no need to dig. There is no gold."

"There has to be," Longarm reasoned. "Your own trackers and those of the Nadene, who are almost as good as a Ute when it comes to tracking the smallest of game across the hardest of earth, have searched for the missing gold. They have found nothing, nor have the greedy whites who also search. There is no other place."

"The man called Long Arm has not seen this. He has not searched. Is Long Arm looking not for gold but for a reason to take up his gun against the Ute?"

67

The politeness was damn sure over now. John Badger made a face and spat onto the ground at his side.

Longarm had no quick answer to that one. John Badger was right, and the Utes knew it. Longarm had come here with an exhumation order already in his pocket and other people's assurances that the missing payroll money had to be in Ouray's grave because it wasn't anyplace else. The simple fact was, he had *not* done any investigating before he came here to talk about digging up the old chief's grave.

"If John Badger is right...if there is no gold in the grave...digging would prove the rightness and honesty of the Utes, and there would be no greedy white men coming here to see for themselves." It was the only response Longarm could think of at the moment. It sounded weak even to him.

"Whoever digs, Long Arm or some other, there must be war."

"Every day that goes by makes it more likely that someone will sneak in and dig," Longarm said.

"No man will dig," Badger said. "No man will live to reach the grave. This I say to you. No man will dig."

"And if I must?"

"No man will dig. Not while yet one of my people lives." Flat. Final. No compromise at all.

As one man, although no signal had been given that Longarm could see, the entire circle of Utes stood. They turned their backs and walked away. Only John Badger was left, standing directly across the fire from Longarm, who now stood too.

The council was ended, but John Badger still had something to say.

"Long Arm's word is true. This is known. And he could have been my brother if his skin was dark or mine was light. Go. Look. Then come back. We will talk again."

It was a hope, faint but nonetheless a measure of hope.

"And in the meantime?" Longarm asked.

"No man will dig until then," John Badger said. "No man will dig after then." John Badger turned on his heels and walked away.

Chapter 9

Longarm sat wolfing beefsteak and fried potatoes. A slab of spicy apple pie was waiting for him when he was done with that. Gray Rock town marshal Jean Briscoe sat across the table from him with a cup of tea before her. Longarm wondered if they had established a habit about this. But the civilized meal tasted mighty good after the rough fare at the agency.

He looked out the window. It was starting to snow, small, hard, gritty flakes of it slanting down into the glass on a driving wind. Longarm grinned. John Badger had been a good dozen hours off on his prediction.

"What is it?" Mrs. Briscoe asked.

"Remembering something. Nothing important."

"Did you see Chipeta when you were out there?"

"Ouray's wife?" He shook his head. "I thought she'd be dead by now. Looked like she had one foot in the grave the last time I saw her, and that was quite a while back."

"She's still alive, all right. Probably living all alone in that house now. I suppose I shouldn't say this where anyone could overhear, the way people are feeling about the Utes right now, but I like Chipeta. I think she had almost as much influence as her husband did for all these years, keeping the peace when things were bad."

"We could use some of that influence right now," Longarm said.

"The Utes think highly of their women. If she isn't

still in mourning, she will be doing whatever she can."

"I hope so." Longarm took a mouthful of steak, chewed, and swallowed. "The folks around here seem to think highly of their women too, Mrs. Briscoe. I hope you're doing everything you can to keep all the damn fools away from the agency. In particular away from that grave."

"I've already talked to everyone I have seen," she assured him. "I tried to make it plain that one person's greed could lead to an uprising." She looked worried. "I don't know how much good it will do, of course, and no one can tell about strangers coming in from the outside. But certainly no one around here wants to see the Utes jump the reservation. I've been trying to get the family people, the ones with the most to lose if that happens, to help keep the others in line. But any one man who thinks he can grab the money and run with his own hide intact . . . well, you just never know what someone might do."

Longarm nodded. "Just so folks know what we're dealing with here."

"The sensible ones do already." She hesitated. "The people here are frightened, Deputy. Some of them are already reacting with bluster, trying to hide their fears from each other, or from themselves. I'm afraid if anything happens between a Ute and the wrong white man, someone might be so scared already that they'll start a fight, and possibly a war, without having anything to do with the grave."

"That bad, is it?"

"Yes," she said. "It is that bad."

"I didn't know that."

She gave him a sad smile. "I don't mean to add to your worries."

"We have enough right now that a few more won't

matter." He grinned. "Seems like it, anyhow."

"What will you do next?"

"Start from the beginning. You did a fine job of it to begin with, but I'll go back to the beginning just like I was investigating the robbery instead of worrying about the Utes. See if I can come up with any new ideas."

"If there is any way I can help..."

Longarm nodded. "I won't hesitate to ask."

Mrs. Briscoe pulled a large turnip-shaped pocketwatch from her handbag and checked the time. "You only have a few minutes until the bank closes," she said.

"Thanks, but I'd rather talk with the banker after hours. Easier then than with customers coming in and out."

Mrs. Briscoe left her tea unfinished on the table and pushed herself away. Longarm stood when she did.

"If you would excuse me, Deputy, I have some things I need to do this afternoon. If you like, I can stop in at the bank and tell Sam that you will be coming to see him."

"I'd appreciate that. Thank you."

They said their goodbyes, and Longarm sat to finish his meal. He would have enjoyed another cup of coffee and a second piece of the excellent pie, but he decided not to take the time. He lighted a cheroot, paid his bill, and turned his coat collar up before stepping out into a sudden storm that was close to the intensity of a blizzard. Next chance he got, he thought, he was going to have to go to the hotel for a heavier coat than the tweed.

Sam Cane must have been watching for him through the bank windows, because by the time Longarm dashed across the street and reached the door someone was there to open it. Longarm was glad about that. The sharp spicules of granulated snow stung when they zipped into the exposed flesh of his cheeks and neck, and he was glad to get indoors again.

"Thanks." Longarm slipped inside and took his hat off, using the flat of the brim to slap the snow from his coat and trousers. In just the hundred yards or so from the restaurant to the bank building he had gotten thoroughly chilled, yet an hour ago he had been almost uncomfortably warm riding back from the agency. Danged if old John Badger hadn't been right after all.

The man who had opened the door for him nodded, if without any show of warmth or welcome, and re-locked the door, pulling the shades down over the glass afterward.

"Mr. Cane?"

"I am."

Longarm introduced himself. Cane shook hands perfunctorily.

The bank vice president—or probably its new president now that Walker Hardifer was dead—was a small man, already balding, although he did not look like he was out of his thirties. Now that business hours were over he had shed his coat and loosened his tie and was working in shirtsleeves and sleeve garters.

Longarm looked around. There was no one else in the bank. He had expected at least one teller to be working on the books. He knew from past experiences that a bank's work is anything but complete at the closing hour, that there was always a great deal of accounting to be done after the day's transactions.

The bank itself was small, a lobby no bigger than ten feet by six with two barred windows facing the lobby. The door into the office was to the left of the

73

windows. In the back there were three desks, the steel safe Marshal Briscoe had told him about, and the immense vault built into the back wall. There were no private offices and no ornamentation unless you wanted to count a calendar and a wall clock.

"I will have to ask you to make this brief, Deputy," Cane said. "I have a great deal of work to do and after the... uh... recent unpleasantness, no one to assist me. My wife expects me home promptly at 6:10."

Recent unpleasantness, Longarm thought. That was one way to put it. Two men were dead; ten if you counted the robbers. That should be unpleasant enough for just about anybody.

"I'll try not to make you late for dinner," Longarm said. He did not really care very much if Sam Cane was late or not. He did not really care very much for Sam Cane. Nothing specific, he just didn't like the man. His attitude, perhaps; the fact that two men he worked with were murdered a few days earlier and now Cane was worried about being home on time.

Cane made no move toward the back part of the bank where the desks and chairs were, so Longarm suggested, "Perhaps we should sit down while we discuss this."

"Will you require that much of my time?"

Longarm smiled at him. It was the kind of smile that had been known to frighten armed felons into giving themselves up to the law. "I hadn't thought so to begin with, Mr. Cane, but it's just possible that this investigation could take a very long time to complete." The smile got wider. "You know how bureaucracies can be, once you get the government involved in things."

Cane remained unruffled, but he seemed to get the

point. He led Longarm into the back of the bank and showed him to a chair.

"May I see your credentials, sir?" Cane asked.

It was an unusual request, but well within Cane's right to ask. Longarm pulled his wallet out and flipped it open. The banker took his time about examining the badge, then asked, "What is your jurisdiction in the matter?"

"Come again?"

"It is my understanding, sir, that bank robbery is a state offense. You are a federal officer. I am asking how this pertains to your jurisdiction."

"The Ute Indians are wards of the federal government. Because of their involvement, the state asked us to handle it."

"The Ute Indians did not rob this bank," Cane said.

"And the state government did not limit my authority when they asked us to take over the case," Longarm said.

In fact, Longarm had no idea how the state had worded its request that the United States Department of Justice become involved. All he really knew about was the exhumation order signed by a federal judge at the state's request. But if Deputy Marshal Custis Long did not know the details, the vice president of a rinky-dink bank in Gray Rock, Colorado wouldn't know them either.

"I see." Cane returned Longarm's wallet and leaned back in his chair with his arms folded across his chest. "What is it you want to know, Deputy Long?"

"Everything. Right from the beginning."

"I have already told everything to Jean Briscoe."

Longarm smiled at the little man. "And now you get to tell it all to me."

Cane sighed. He sounded exasperated. Still, he

seemed to realize finally that the tall federal deputy was not going to leave and let him get back to work until the story was told. Speaking in a monotone, sounding almost bored, Cane retold the same tale Longarm had already heard from Mrs. Briscoe.

"I came to some time after the robbers left," Cane concluded. "My injuries were treated by Dr. Hauser. Here, not in his office. I went home. I still have not caught up with all the work left undone as a result."

Evidence of the injuries was still obvious, although the man's bruises had yellowed and were fading. A line of dark stitches crossed his scalp above where his hairline should have been. Lucky for Sam, Longarm thought, that he was going bald. The doc didn't have to shave his head before he could sew it. There certainly was no question, though, that the man had been beaten. And at the time, from a gash in the scalp like that, there would have been an awful lot of blood. It was entirely reasonable to suppose that the robbers had left him for dead.

"What about the money?" Longarm asked.

Cane rummaged around among the papers on his desk and found the one he wanted. "Eighty one thousand four hundred dollars," he said. "Exactly."

"Mostly double eagles?" Longarm was trying to work out a rough idea of how much bulk and weight would be involved with a load of gold coins that large. It would certainly be considerable, he knew.

"None of it was in coin, Deputy. I assumed you knew that already."

"Currency?" Longarm was more than surprised. He was damned well amazed.

Cane nodded.

"What about serial numbers?"

"None recorded," Cane said. "The bank has always

been understaffed. Even before . . . this. Besides, it was not felt to be necessary. There has never . . . *had* never been a robbery of the Gray Rock Bank."

"You said this was payroll money for the Halleluia Mine, I believe."

Cane nodded smugly. "Payroll and certain other expenditures would be my understanding. If you wish further information about those you would have to contact the management of the Halleluia directly. It would not be my place to divulge such information."

"But you said it was currency, not coin, making up this payroll."

Cane nodded again.

"Mr. Cane, I don't mean to be argumentative here, but everybody knows that miners want their pay in gold coin. They don't trust currency. They want hard money for their work and preferably the same metal they're taking out of the ground, whether they're mining silver or gold."

Cane still looked smug. "That may be true elsewhere, Deputy Long, but here they had the choice of being paid in currency or not being paid at all."

"Why was that?"

"Walker Hardifer was a wise and careful man, Deputy. Currency is considerably lighter than coin. He was able to achieve a significant savings in transportation costs, savings for the bank *and* for its depositors, by dealing only in currency when bulk shipments of cash were made."

"What about the mine owners? Didn't they care?"

Cane spread his hands and almost smiled. "Bank policy on the matter was clear. Of course they had the option to obtain coin elsewhere, in which case shipping and insurance would have been their own responsibility. They wisely chose to deal in currency."

Damned unusual, Longarm thought, but reasonable enough if the man in charge of the bank was more interested in playing the skinflint than pleasing his customers. And apparently Walker Hardifer had been in the driver's seat since he had the only bank in town.

"What about insurance covering the loss?" Longarm asked.

"The bank does, of course, provide insurance coverage against theft. Although I daresay our premium rates are likely to rise now."

"It was the bank's loss, though, not the mine's?"

Cane nodded. "A representative of the Halleluia management, with guards, was en route to the bank when the robbery occurred. The guards, I believe, were fully armed, and were among those who opened fire on the fleeing thieves."

"But the bank was closed."

"Common policy in all sensible banking institutions is to conduct major cash transactions within private, controlled surroundings."

Longarm grunted. He lighted another cheroot, ignoring Cane's scowl when he did so, and thought for a moment. "How large was the money taken, Cane? The physical bulk of it, I mean, not the amount."

Cane had to think about that one. After a moment he gestured in the air with his soft, uncallused palms. "Approximately the size of five common building bricks," he said. "Most of the denominations were large. All of the bills had been counted, stacked, and banded before shipment to us."

Longarm grunted again. In a way, this complicated things. A heap of money about the size of five bricks was a hell of a lot easier to hide than eighty thousand in gold coin.

But in another way, he realized, it could help. If

the searchers had been looking for a large mass of loot, they might easily have overlooked hiding places small enough to contain the money that had been stolen.

"Thank you for your time, Mr. Cane." Longarm stood. Cane did not offer to shake hands, and neither did the deputy. "I hope you make it home for supper on time," Longarm told Cane.

"Thank you."

Cane followed him to the front door and let him out. Longarm heard the distinctive snick of the bolt being thrown closed behind him, and the banker went back to his dreary chores.

Chapter 10

Longarm ran back to the hotel and skidded into the lobby with relief. He had been running with the wind this time, the blowing spicules of snow at his back, so he was not quite so uncomfortable as he had been, but he was still glad to be indoors.

A drink would have been mighty welcome, but he had no time for personal pleasures yet. There was too much at stake here for loafing.

He checked the Ingersoll from his vest pocket and saw that he had plenty of time before the Halleluia offices would be expected to close, even if it was well past banking hours now. Before he headed out into the weather again, though, he went upstairs to his room and exchanged his light suit coat for the much warmer sheepskin coat he carried folded in his bag. Long experience had taught him to carry a heavy coat and gloves with him when he traveled the high country regardless of the time of year, and obviously this western slope semi-desert was as unpredictable as the San Juans that lay to the east.

He jammed a cheroot between his teeth, pulled his gloves on, and buttoned the collar of his coat high around his throat before going out again into the cold gale.

The Halleluia lay immediately north of the town, about a quarter-mile walk uphill toward the dome of gray granite that gave the town its name. The shafts of the mine would be sunk into that granite, Longarm knew. Gold is not found in the more common native sandstone but is frequently present in quartz-laced granite.

Rather than go to the time and trouble of getting a horse from the livery, Longarm pulled his Stetson low on his forehead and turtled deep into the sheepskin-lined collar of his coat. The cold wind was still uncomfortable, but it was bearable now, and he made the journey at a mighty fast walk.

Snow blowing almost horizontal to the ground made visibility difficult from any distance of more than a few yards, but when he neared the vertical pile of buildings and towers that housed the Halleluia Longarm was able to see a low building separate from the rest of the structure which he assumed was the office. He opened the door and stepped inside, out of the wind, without waiting for an invitation.

"Whew!" He tilted his hat back a fraction of an inch and let the coat collar down. "Are you the manager?"

The bookish-looking man at the larger of the two desks in the office shook his head. "Accounts clerk," he said. "The boss is up at the mine."

"Damn."

Longarm got a sympathetic grin from the fellow. "There's a path outside, all the way to the top, but if you don't mind risking some dirt you can climb up through the separator and crusher shacks. Just stay out of the bottom-most building. That's the amalgamating room. Visitors aren't welcome there." He said the last part with a smile of apology rather than a threat.

Longarm nodded. He was familiar enough with this kind of hardrock mining. At the top would be the shaft opening with its hoists going deep into the rock. It was there that the gold ore would be hauled from underground.

From there, built with one structure beneath the next so that gravity could do the work of movement as the ore was processed, would come the crusher where the ore would be broken from rock into granulated dust, then the separator where non-metallic rock would be discarded from the process with chemicals, and then the amalgamator where the valuable ores would be concentrated with heat and mercury into a concentrated "sponge" ready for shipment to a refinery. The resulting sponge was not pure gold, but it was a concentrate pure enough to be worth shipping costs for final sale to the refinery. The ore itself from a formation like this would be so thinly laced with valuable metals, contain so much waste rock, that it would not be worth stealing.

Longarm left the office and ran uphill past the amalgamating shack and found a ladder leading up to the separator.

Two men were working there, one picking out pieces of rock too large to go into the chemical flotation vat while the other used a rake to pull crushed ore down a chute into the vat. The place smelled of chemicals, the odor giving an illusion of heat even though the building was unheated and plenty cold. The men who were working there seemed cheerful enough. They nodded pleasantly at Longarm, and the sorter stepped aside so Longarm could climb the indoor ladder—it was too steep to be considered a stairway—into the next level.

There too the men were cheerful enough. The steam-driven stamp mill, small steel feet driven up and down by way of rods and rollers to crush the broken rock under them, was entirely too noisy to permit conversation. They waved a polite hello, and Longarm edged past the greasy machinery to reach the ladder up to the hoist level.

Here more men were at work, one operating the steam-driven hoist elevator to bring ore or miners up from underground, another sorting the blast-shattered rock, putting gold ore in one pile for a third man to shovel it down the chute to the crusher and tossing the unwanted granite down another chute that led to the tailings dump outside.

"Can I help you?" the hoist operator asked.

"I'm looking for the boss."

"Down below," the hoist man said. "Is it important?"

Longarm pulled out his wallet and showed the fellow his badge.

The hoist operator grinned. "I ain't done it, Marshal."

Longarm laughed. If he had had any suspicions that the Halleluia mine workers were disgruntled, the suspicions certainly would seem to be laid to rest by this crowd.

The hoist man cocked his head and eyed Longarm's polished boots and unsoiled trousers. "Dressed like that, Marshal, I reckon you won't want to go underground. Just a minute and I'll call the boss up."

"Thanks."

The hoist operator leaned forward past the row of levers that controlled the elevator and gave a series of tugs on a cord connected to a bell. Longarm knew that there would be another, matching bell far underground at the other end of that cord. The hoistmen at either end of the bell signals could pass messages by way of prearranged codes based on the number of rings and their timing. Obviously these were old hands at the Halleluia, long used to their jobs. Mines with rapid turnover of personnel usually kept a card or sign posted showing the signals so there would be no chance of error. A misunderstood bell signal could kill people.

There was a delay underground, then an answering bell signal. Longarm had no idea what the signal meant.

"How far down are they?" he asked.

"Sixteen hundred feet." The bell rang again, a longer signal this time. "Excuse me," the hoistman said. He pulled on one lever and pushed another forward, and the drum-wound cable began to turn. "This won't be what you could call real speedy," the hoistman said.

At least ten minutes went by before the elevator platform reached ground level. The steel-floored cage held a pile of shattered ore and, perched on top of the ore pile, two mud-spattered, filthy miners wearing rubber boots and cloth caps.

The miners stepped off the elevator, and the hoistman jerked a thumb over his shoulder toward Longarm. "Fella here to see you, Jerry."

Longarm had no idea which of the muddy men was the boss of the Halleluia until one of them stepped forward, rubbed his palm carefully over his muddy jeans, and extended the hand to shake. "Jerry Peak," he said with a smile.

Longarm introduced himself.

"You'd be here about the robbery, then." Peak nodded. "C'mon down to the office where we'll be more comfortable, an' I'll tell you whatever you want to know."

"Good." Longarm would be glad enough to get back down to the protection of the office building. The wind was harder up here against the side of the granite dome, and both sharp wind and stinging granules of hard snow were coming into the hoist shack through the wall cutout that led down to the tailings dump. Peak led the way back down the ladders.

On the way down, Longarm had a chance to get a better look at the Halleluia's boss. Jerry Peak was of average height and had a wiry toughness about him. His hair was pale under a liberal coating of mud where the cap did not cover. Except for that handshake and introduction there would have been no way in the world a stranger could have guessed him to be not just another mine employee.

As they passed from one level to the next the men working there either greeted their boss with a casual wave or an insulting, laughing comment or, if they were busy, ignored him in favor of their work. Poor relations between workers and management was not a problem at the Halleluia.

When they got back to the office, Peak swept a pile of newspapers from a chair onto the floor and motioned that Longarm should take the seat. He shivered. "I could stand something to warm the belly, Marshal. How 'bout you?"

Longarm nodded.

The clerk in the office was busy transferring figures from scraps of soiled paper into a neat ledger. Peak did not bother the man but went to a cabinet himself and poured two drinks from a fancily labeled bottle. He handed one to Longarm and went around to the other side of the smaller desk in the office to take his own seat. "Rye is all I've got, Marshal. Hope it'll do."

Longarm grinned. "A man after my own heart."

Peak winked at him. He took a healthy swallow of the whiskey and sighed.

When Longarm drank he discovered that the rye

was mellow with age, as good as he had ever had. "You do know how to make a fellow comfortable, Mr. Peak," he said.

"Hell, call me Jerry. Mr. Peak was my daddy."

"All right. And I'm Longarm to my friends."

"Longarm it is, then. Now, what can I do for you?"

"Like you already guessed, I want to know about the robbery, whatever you know about it, and the money that was stolen. A payroll, was it?"

Jerry took another slug of the fine rye. "Part payroll, part bonus, and part of it payment for a new steam engine," he said. "We need to upgrade the hoist, you see. Put something in that's faster. Right now our production's limited by the time it takes to haul the ore up to the surface an' get it started on the concentrating process. A faster hoist will let us increase production, oh, forty percent, I'd say. Ralph," he pointed toward the clerk who was still bent over his books, "claims forty one point five percent."

"You don't always have that much cash to be picked up, then?"

Jerry shook his head. "Generally a lot less."

"Who would have known about the increase that time?"

The mine boss—Longarm still was not sure about the man's exact position here—thought about that for a moment. "Me, of course. My wife. Ralph. The steam-engine salesman. An' anybody he might have told. You know how drummers are. He's a friendly sort an' likes to do business in a saloon. Could've told about anybody, I reckon."

"What about the stockholders, the mine owners?"

Jerry Peak grinned. "I already listed them all for you. Me and my missus, we own the Halleluia outright. Found enough high-grade near the top to finance

86

the rest of 'er. Had to work like hell to get her going that way, but I'll double-damn-guarantee you, Longarm, we shouted Halleluia when we got 'er done. Did my own drilling, Emily holdin' the drill an' me swingin' the singlejack. Packed powder an' blew in the afternoon, an' then half the night I'd be swinging a hammer to break the rock while Em picked the ore by hand afterward. Made enough that way, though, to buy some equipment, and she's just kinda grew since then." He was still grinning. The man was proud of himself, and Longarm figured he had plenty of reason to be.

In spite of the man's open, friendly manner, though, Longarm could not help realizing that by robbing the bank himself, or arranging to have it done when all that cash would be on hand, Jerry Peak would have picked up a tidy bonus for the Halleluia mine.

"I take it the Halleluia won't suffer any loss because of the robbery," Longarm said.

Jerry shook his head. "Nope. Woulda, of course, if we'd already taken delivery of the money, but we hadn't. As she stands, the bank's insurance will cover it all."

"So the miners will still be paid?"

"Already have been. I wired to Durango right away for enough to cover the payroll. They sent it in special. The rest is s'posed to be on the way from Denver some time in the next week." Peak chuckled. "By mail, matter of fact. That way you boys will do the guardin' for me."

"You said there was some bonus money included in the amount, I believe."

Jerry nodded. "I pay two dollars a day. That's pretty much the standard wage. But the boys know when things are going good, Em and me declare a

87

bonus an' give them some extra now an' then. Hell, Longarm, me and Em got more money right now than we could spend in a lifetime, and we got no children to pass it on to. Not for lack of trying, but we ain't been blessed. So time to time we show the boys we appreciate the work they're doing to make us rich."

The clerk, Ralph, turned his head and injected something into the conversation for the first time. "Damn fool here goes and doubles the wages two, three times a year. I try to tell him he's being an ass, but he does it anyway." Ralph was smiling when he said that. Obviously his wage was among those that was doubled now and then, and he liked it.

No wonder the Halleluia did not have a high turnover among its workers, Longarm thought.

Longarm got back to the business at hand. "What about the time you were supposed to pick the money up, Jerry? I understand you were running a little late that day."

Peak shrugged. "The time lock opens at 3:10. Walker always wanted us there at 3:15 or a little earlier, but you know how it is. We always got to let the boys clean up a mite," he grinned, "an' me too for that matter, an' get the guns passed around for guard purposes. Then whatever of us can be spared from work hike down and get the money. We ain't all that much on watching the clock so sometimes we're a mite late."

"Mostly late," Ralph chided. "I keep after him, Marshal, but he doesn't listen to me. I think Jerry was on time once last February. And that was only because the hoist fouled and there wasn't anything better to do right then."

Longarm chatted with the mine owner a while longer, but it looked as if there was little enough to be learned here. *If* Jerry Peak was telling him the truth. There was still the possibility that Peak might have arranged to give himself a bonus too. But there were some ways Longarm could look into that possibility.

Eventually Longarm drained his third glass of the excellent rye and stood to shake hands with Peak. "Thanks for all your help, Jerry."

"Sure thing, Longarm. Anything else you think of, you can find me here in the daytime or at home otherwise. Em and me don't go out much."

Longarm nodded and prepared to leave, pulling his coat and gloves on.

"Longarm."

"Yeah, Jerry?"

"I hope you find whoever shot Walker an' Jimmy. Old Walker was tight as a tick's asshole, but Jimmy was a pretty good kid."

It was a damned strange thing for the man to say, considering that all of the robbers were already dead and buried. Longarm reminded Peak of that.

"Marshal, I might be just an old underground miner, but I'm not entirely stupid. The fact that you're here and asking the questions you been asking, you think somebody put that crowd up to the robbery. Could be pure accident, of course, that they happened to hit the Gray Rock Bank on the day they did an' at the time they did. But if you're right an' somebody tipped them to it, I figure that somebody is as guilty as them for the murders. And if you're right, well, I hope to hell you find 'em and do 'em under."

Longarm had a last-second thought and asked one more question, thinking that if there was gold this close to the Los Pinos Agency, perhaps there was gold *on* the reservation too. "How do you stand on the Utes, Jerry?"

"Peaceable, Marshal. An' so are my boys. Close as they are, if the Utes decide to jump that reservation an' start taking scalps, we're out of business for a spell."

Longarm grunted and turned his coat collar high. He thanked Peak again and stepped outside. But now, after not more than two hours of near-blizzard conditions, the wind had died off and the sky was already clearing.

Below him the town of Gray Rock and the land around it were a patchwork crazy quilt of drifted snow and wind-scoured bare ground.

Longarm lighted a cheroot and walked back down to the town at an easy pace.

Chapter 11

"What next?" Jean Briscoe asked. For a change she was joining Longarm at mealtime. She had tried to order the inexpensive special at the hotel restaurant, but Longarm, intending to pay for both meals, talked her into a steak instead. She seemed to be enjoying it as a special treat after the cheap food she must have been living on lately.

"Pie, I think. It's pretty good here," he told her.

She smiled. "You know what I meant."

"Go out and see if I can come up with any ideas about where the money is hidden, I guess. The Utes insist it isn't in old Ouray's grave, even though everybody says that's where it has to be. But I pretty much promised John Badger that I'd go look for myself. So I have to do it."

"You won't find anything."

"That's what everyone tells me."

"Still, I do see your problem. And if you told him you would go, you certainly have to do so."

"Badger admitted right out that they have a faction of young bucks out there who want an excuse to go to war again. Probably figure they got the short end of things last year and are pining for a chance to even the score this time around. So at this point any kind of lie from a federal officer might be all the excuse they would need."

"Will you go in the morning?"

He nodded and wiped the last trace of gravy from his plate with half a biscuit. "First light."

"I see." She toyed with the remnants of food left on her plate, pushing them around with the tines of her fork.

"You had a reason for asking that, didn't you?"

"Nothing that I can't handle myself."

"But you'd rather not." It was not really a question. Mrs. Briscoe shrugged.

"Tell me about it," Longarm invited.

"It isn't really important," she insisted.

Longarm smiled. "Then it won't hurt if you tell me what it is."

He got a smile from her in return. "All right. It is just that I have this paper to serve. A court order. And the man is known to be...unpleasant at times. I'm afraid when he sees this—it's a writ of divorcement— he might do something he shouldn't."

"He doesn't know?"

"He thinks his wife ran away to her sister's. Certainly she had good enough reason to. He used to beat her, quite badly, every time he got drunk. Which was several times a week. As far as I know he is expecting her to come crawling back to him any day now, but she went to Durango and filed papers for a legal divorce. She is a good woman, Longarm. She certainly would not have felt right about just walking out and leaving him. As far as that goes, she didn't feel right about asking for a divorce either. She cried on my shoulder before she got out of town. Stayed overnight with me until the stage was ready, actually. The only reason I was able to talk her into filing the papers is their little girl. She's just four. He was starting to hit the child too, and Linda couldn't bear that. I think

92

she would have stayed if he had only been beating her, but when he started on the girl she felt she had to leave."

Longarm frowned. If there was anything worse than a grown man who would hit a woman, it had to be a grown man who would beat up on a kid. "I don't know of any law that says writs can't be served after office hours," he said.

"What?"

"I mean, I still want to get away at first light tomorrow. But there's no reason in the world why I can't serve that paper for you tonight."

"Would you?" She sounded relieved. More than likely she had been thinking it would be her turn to be beaten by this fellow if she served the paper herself. She might well have been right about that too, Longarm thought. But he was sure willing to see how the man reacted when there was another male facing him.

"I don't really have the authority to do it as a federal officer," he said, "but I don't see any reason why you couldn't deputize me as a temporary Gray Rock officer. Nothing in the law to prohibit that either, far as I know." He smiled and winked. "What are you paying?"

Mrs. Briscoe laughed. "Dessert?"

"Fair enough. We'll come back here and have it after I've done the work."

"Thank you, Longarm."

He left a tip and asked the waiter to put the meals on his hotel bill. It was easier to pay with a government voucher that way instead of cutting into his cash. Then he followed Jean Briscoe across the street to her office.

She lighted a lamp and found the writ in the paperwork in her desk. She handed it to Longarm.

"Do you want to use a shotgun or anything?"

He shook his head. "No need to endanger anybody but the gentleman in question, particularly if he's not at home."

"At this time of evening I would expect to find him in the Red Garter." She blushed a little when she mentioned the name of the establishment. "Should I go with you?"

"No, I'd rather you go back to the hotel and wait for me. I'll be by shortly to collect my pay."

"All right." Impulsively she laid a hand on his wrist and squeezed. "Thanks."

Longarm saw her back to the porch of the hotel, then turned and walked down the street in the direction of the Red Garter. The saloon, and whatever more it might have been, was at the western edge of the town. He had noticed the sign when he rode out to the agency the day before.

As he walked he read over the court order to find the name of the man he wanted.

The Red Garter was pretty much the kind of place its name would lead a man to expect. One side of the room was taken up by a well-attended bar that was doing a brisk trade. On the other side of the room were a faro table and roulette wheel and other tables for card playing. A piano sat silent and unused at the back of the place.

The entertainment, and probably other services as well, was being provided by a foursome of powdered and rouged women who were circulating among the customers cadging drinks and free feels.

A close look showed that the women were not particularly attractive, but their manner of dress was certainly eye-catching. Probably no one ever noticed that the whores themselves were a bunch of aging dogs.

Their dresses were all short, red, flouncy things that showed plenty of powdered tit at the top end and stockinged, red-gartered leg at the bottom.

What really got the attention, though, was when any of them turned around.

There was no back to the dresses. None at all.

Each of them wore a lacy black contraption of some sort to hold their stockings up, and there were a few lacy red straps behind their waists and shoulders to hold the otherwise unsupported fronts of their dresses in place.

Except for those few wisps of elastic they were all naked when viewed from the rear.

Longarm supposed he should have been all kinds of aroused by the display, but he was not. The woman nearest him had pimples on her butt. Maybe that had something to do with his lack of response.

He ignored the entertainment and went to the bar.

"What'll you have, mister?"

"Stanley Fisher," Longarm said. "I have a message for him."

The barman scowled. "What kind of message?"

"Are you Stanley Fisher?"

"Not me, mister."

"Then I don't guess the message is for you, is it?"

"Fuck off."

The bartender turned and tried to walk away toward the other end of his bar. Longarm's hand clamped onto the front of the man's shirt had something to do with the fact that he did not go very far.

Longarm dragged the man halfway across the bar until they were nose to nose. He smiled at the barman, but it was not an encouraging expression.

"We don't have to do this the easy way," Longarm said in a mild tone. "If you'd rather, I can start turning your customers upside down and chucking them out of here until I get to the one I want. Or you can introduce me to Mr. Fisher. Your choice." The voice was mild, but Longarm's iron grip shifted from the man's shirt to his throat and applied pressure.

"I think I see Stan right over there."

"Thank you." Longarm released him, helped him stand upright on the proper side of the bar, and smoothed down the front of his shirt. "I do appreciate your help, neighbor."

The bartender seemed more than willing to pretend that nothing unusual had occurred. He turned his head and bellowed, "Stan! Fella here to see you." The barman turned away and began busily refilling mugs with sour-smelling beer.

The man who responded to the call had been in the process of feeling the bare rump of one of the women. He let go of her, wiped his hand on the front of her dress, and came over to the bar.

"Yeah?" He sounded and looked as if he was in a perpetual state of the grumps. Dour expression, narrow dark eyes, and a drooping, scraggly moustache. He needed a shave and some serious dental work. He also carried a small nickel-plated revolver in the waistband of his trousers. Longarm had always thought that a mighty uncertain place to carry such an important tool . . . but then he knew some almighty slick hands with a gun who favored the method. It was certainly not grounds for assuming the man was slow. "Who the hell are you?" Fisher squinted at him. "I don't know you, mister."

Too late to do anything about it, Longarm realized that neither he nor Jean Briscoe had remembered to deputize him as a Gray Rock officer after they got to her office.

"Deputy marshal," Longarm said, careful not to

specify just what kind of marshal he was a deputy for. "I have a writ to serve on Stanley L. Fisher."

"That ain't me," Fisher said. He spun around and headed for the front door.

"Fisher!"

The man stopped and half turned back toward Longarm. He had an ugly look about him. Oddly, then, his expression softened into a smirking smile.

To both sides of Fisher, men's eyes shifted suddenly from the confrontation between the two men to a point somewhere behind Longarm's back.

Longarm did not wait for any better warning than that. He ducked and whirled, and an oak bungstarter whistled through the empty space his head had just vacated.

The damn bartender had tried to bat Longarm's head off.

Longarm's left hand slashed out while his right was already going for the Colt.

The edge of his hand connected just where he wanted it to, on the barman's throat, and the bartender dropped out of sight behind his bar.

Longarm turned his attention back to Fisher. Fisher had the shiny revolver in his fist, pointed more or less toward the deputy while he groped for the hammer.

"Let it be, Fisher."

He got the little gun cocked and tried to take aim at Longarm's head.

It is a fool's move to try to shoot at any part of an armed man except the largest part. Longarm triggered the big Colt and shot Stanley Fisher in the belly. His second shot took the man in the chest and toppled him face forward into the sawdust scattered on the Red Garter's floor.

Fisher knocked over an empty chair and a spittoon

when he fell. The spittoon dumped over onto its side, covering Fisher's ear and face with its contents. Fisher did not mind; he was already dead.

Longarm kept the smoking Colt pointed to cover the crowd in the place and backed around until he could look into the area behind the bar.

The bartender was sitting on the floor, leaning against the back of the bar with both hands clutching his throat. His face was almost as red as the dress fronts the women were wearing, but he looked like nothing had been seriously damaged inside his throat. He was breathing, anyway.

"Get up," Longarm told him.

The bartender shook his head and tried to wave Longarm away. He was making gagging noises.

"That wasn't an invitation, neighbor. You're on your way to jail."

The barman shook his head vigorously from side to side.

"The charge is obstructing an officer in the performance of his duties. If you want to disagree you're welcome to get a lawyer an' tell it all to a judge, but until then, neighbor, you either come along with me or your buddies will have to carry you out of there in a big box."

The bartender got to his feet this time and meekly allowed Longarm to lead him out of the Red Garter and down the street toward the jail. Longarm hoped there was someone else around to take over the bar, or the Red Garter was going to serve an awful lot of free drinks for the rest of the night.

Chapter 12

"Did Fisher have any insurance? On his life, I mean," Longarm said. They were back at the hotel restaurant, but neither one of them was in the mood any longer for pie. Jean Briscoe was having tea, and Longarm had coffee, although he might have preferred something stronger.

"I don't know. Why?"

"It occurs to me that the order was never actually served on him. He didn't give me a chance. And, aside from the fact that the man died not knowing that his wife had divorced him, if I understand things right the divorce might not have been really final—official and everything—until or unless that paper was legally served. What I was thinking is, if this Fisher fellow had any insurance on his life, it would now be payable to his widow. Probably not, though, if the paper had ever been served. You might want to look into that for the sake of your friend and her little girl."

"I shall."

Jean Briscoe sipped her tea and gave Longarm a close look. "You really are a nice man, aren't you?"

Longarm smiled at her. "That's the sort of thing a man can't hardly have an answer to unless he wants to come across either awful stupid or awful stuck on himself. But I thank you."

"I meant it, you know."

"And I thank you."

She paused. "Could I discuss something with you that is . . . personal?"

"Of course. Whatever it is, ma'am, it won't go a step beyond this table," he promised.

"I would prefer that you call me Jean, then. If you wouldn't mind."

"Of course, Jean."

"I . . . Oh, I don't know how to say this. Maybe I should just be quiet."

"Whatever is comfortable."

She sighed. "Ever since Linda Fisher left town I haven't anyone I can really confide in. Except Button, of course, and this isn't the sort of thing I could talk to *him* about."

"Button?"

"My son. Oh, that's right, you haven't met him. I should have realized." She sighed again. "His name is really Burton, Burton Junior, but we always called him Button. I suppose he will be wanting me to stop that soon. He's twelve now. Am I boring you?"

"Not at all."

"He's a wonderful little boy, but he isn't taking his father's death well. And he never has been really healthy. He has always been frail. Which is the biggest reason we can't seem . . . couldn't even when Burton was alive, that is . . . can't seem to get ahead. There have always been medical expenses, that sort of thing. Not that I regret a bit of it. He is a dear little boy."

Longarm nodded.

"Tonight he's spending the night with one of his friends. He was so excited I thought he was going to make himself sick and not be able to go. He wanted to go so badly I think he would have even if he did make himself sick. That's why I'm free this evening. Otherwise I would be at home with him. Ever since

Burton died, Button has been my whole life." She sighed.

Longarm was beginning to get an idea of what the problem might be. "Everybody needs a break from responsibility now and then," he said gently. "You don't have to feel guilty about it."

"I guess I do, a little," she admitted.

"You shouldn't," he said. "You are a healthy, attractive, normal human being, Jean. There's no reason in the world you should feel bad about feeling relieved to have an evening free from responsibility."

She sighed deeply. "If that was all it was, I think I could manage," she said.

"Oh?"

"Did you mean what you said just now?" she asked.

"Which?"

"About me being . . . attractive?" She was not looking at him now. She was playing with the spoon lying beside her teacup, and she was blushing.

"Yes, I very much meant that, Jean. You are a mighty attractive woman, and I daresay some smart man is going to get himself a real jewel when he hooks up with you."

She snorted. "That will be the day."

"Sooner than you might think," Longarm told her. "You are pretty, you are bright, and I suspect you are completely loyal. I don't know what more a man could want."

"I am not young any more, Longarm. I have a son who needs constant care and medical attention. I have neither land nor money to bring to a man. Why would any man want the likes of me?"

"Any man smart enough to see all of what you have to offer would want you, Jean. Believe me. It's true."

She shook her head.

"Wait and see. You might not think it now, but I'll be proven right about it."

She squeezed her eyes closed, and Longarm thought he could see the beginning of a tear. "The worst part of it is that I'm so damned *healthy*, as you put it. And it makes me feel so *guilty*."

"I don't know what you mean." It was the truth. He honestly did not yet.

"I don't know why I should be telling you all this. Except that you are such a nice man and so understanding. And you are a stranger in Gray Rock. As soon as your job is done here you will be gone, and I won't see you again."

"Sometimes that does make it easier to talk," he said. "And you don't have to worry about me repeating anything in some other town either. I wouldn't do that to you."

"I believe you." She wiped at her eyes and gave him a small smile.

She sighed. "Burton was a wonderful husband. I know women are not supposed to feel this way, but...he was wonderful...at night...too." She was blushing furiously now. "If you know what I mean."

This time he did. He nodded, not wanting to say anything that might make her uncomfortable.

"Since Burton died..." She could not finish the sentence.

"I understand."

Jean Briscoe took in a deep, shuddering breath. She gathered her courage and blurted, "Would you...I mean...would it to be too much trouble..." This last phrase cut through the anxiety she was feeling, and in spite of herself she began to laugh at the way it sounded. "I *am* a silly creature, aren't I?"

"Not at all, Jean. And in answer to the question you've been trying to ask, I would feel honored and very happy to share your company."

She smiled at him. "That is a nice way for you to put it, Longarm. Thank you." She hesitated. "One thing, though."

"Yes?"

"I am not really comfortable with nicknames for grown men. What is your first name again?"

"Custis," he said with a smile.

"Thank you, Custis." She stood and placed a coin on the table. His fee for serving the paper on Stanley Fisher. "Would you . . . walk me home now?"

"My pleasure, Jean."

The house was small and not very well built. It was filled with too much furniture, furniture much too large for the three tiny rooms. Longarm guessed that the house was rented but the furniture had come from the home Burton Briscoe had had to sell after his accident.

Jean lighted the lamps in the living room and in the kitchen. In a small voice she offered coffee.

"No, thanks." He placed a hand gently on her shoulder. She dropped her eyes and blushed.

Longarm understood her dilemma. She felt a mature woman's strong physical needs. But there was still within her an equally strong sense of loyalty and fidelity to a man who was now dead and who would never again take her in his arms to comfort and please her.

"If you'd rather not, Jean, it's all right."

Her answer was to come to him, slipping inside the protection of his arms and placing her head against his chest. Her arms crept around him and he thought, oddly, that what she seemed to be doing now was breathing in the sharp, masculine scents of his body.

For a moment she clutched at him with a fierce strength, then relaxed and swayed back a few inches so she could look up into his eyes. Apparently she had reached her decision now. She smiled.

He kissed her.

He had intended the kiss to be gentle, friendly rather than passionate until she was fully relaxed and comfortable with him, but this was no shy, inexperienced young girl. She was a woman grown, and once her decision was reached there were no more hesitations. She was quite willing now to set the tone of the evening.

She kissed him hungrily, her tongue probing immediately into his mouth, her belly pressing and grinding against his groin.

Longarm's reaction was automatic. He stiffened, and she must have felt the change through the layers of cloth that separated them. She broke off the kiss and tilted her head back to smile at him with obvious pleasure.

"You've had something to drink," she said, "and been smoking those cigars."

"Do you mind?"

She shook her head quickly. "I like it. It's been too long." She kissed him again, even harder now, and said, "I like the taste of you. I want the flavors of you as well as the feel of you. Would you mind?"

"No."

Smiling still, she took him by the hand and led him with her through the two small rooms while she blew out the lamps first in the living room and then in the kitchen. She led him into the dark bedroom.

She let go of his hand and left him standing there

104

in the unfamiliar surroundings while she carefully closed the bedroom door and pulled the curtains shut.

"Would you mind if I light the lamp?" she asked. "I would like to see you, Custis. I want to be able to look at you."

"I wouldn't mind."

He heard the scrape of a match and saw its flare. She raised the globe of a small bedside lamp and lighted the wick.

The bedroom was as heavily furnished as the other two rooms. The bedstead was huge, and there was a massive wardrobe of dark wood occupying most of one wall. A small cot, tidily made up now, was against the opposite wall. That would be where the boy slept, Longarm guessed. There was little floor space left. The bed was a brass four-poster with a fluffy down coverlet over it and a mountain of covered pillows at the head. This would be the bed she had shared for so long with her husband. Longarm wondered if he should have taken her to his hotel room instead, where there would be no lingering memories. But it was here she had wanted to bring him. Perhaps this choice was what she needed so she could break with the past and begin looking toward the future.

"I like what I see here," Longarm said. He was looking at her, not at the bedroom.

She smiled and without hesitation began to remove the many layers of clothing a respectable woman was expected to wear. Longarm took his coat off and laid it on the foot of the empty cot.

"Wait," she said. "Let me."

He nodded and waited for her.

Naked, she was better looking than he might have expected. Her breasts were full and sagged only slightly, their nipples large and dark. Her hips were round beneath a surprisingly slim waist, and her belly was nearly flat. Her skin was pale and smooth and looked very soft. She had little pubic hair. What there was of it looked at first glance to be much paler than her hair. Then he realized that it was graying much faster than elsewhere, giving her an almost blonde appearance there in the light from the one small lamp.

She reached up to remove the pins from her hair and gave her head a small shake, sending a spill of gray-shot dark hair down over her shoulders. Longarm liked the effect the movement had on her breasts.

He smiled. "You are very lovely," he said.

Jean smiled and came to him. She seemed perfectly comfortable, even pleased, when he looked at her.

Her eyes went to the bulge of jutting cloth below his belt, but it was his tie she reached for.

He let her undress him. She did it slowly, her fingers lingering and caressing as they worked at the knots and the buttons.

He allowed her to remove his gunbelt and saw that without being asked she rebuckled the belt and draped it over a corner of the bedpost where his head would be. She had, after all, been married to a peace officer.

She knelt to help him off with his boots and remained there, kneeling at his feet on the uncovered hardwood floor, to strip off his socks and trousers and drawers.

When Longarm was naked, she rocked back on her heels and spent several long moments just looking at him, her eyes roving over his lean, scarred frame.

"Yes," she said in a throaty whisper.

She reached up with one gentle hand and ran her fingertips lightly over his chest and belly, looking but not yet touching elsewhere.

Longarm was throbbingly erect, but he wanted to

be patient with her, to give her this time at her own pace and for her own pleasure.

She took his hand and tugged him down into a sitting position on the side of the big bed.

Still kneeling, she parted his knees and crept in between them. She turned away for a moment to adjust the wick of the lamp to get a better flame so she could examine him the better.

Jean sighed. Finally, delicately, she touched him, lightly running the fingertips of both hands up and down the length of him.

"Yes," she whispered again. She sounded hoarse, almost choked. Longarm waited, willing to let her take this as she wished.

She leaned close, and he could feel the soft, warm exhalations of her breath as she smelled of his male flesh.

She steadied him with the light touch of one hand, stilling the quick, rhythmic pounding of his cock as each heartbeat jounced the tip up and down.

Holding him lightly near the base to keep him still, she pressed first one cheek and then the other against the bulbous red head. She seemed to want to absorb him with all of her senses.

Longarm stroked the back of her head gently, careful not to pull her forward—the initiative was to be hers this night—but wanting to soothe and pet her.

Her free hand came up to toy with his balls, and with her other hand she pushed his cock upright.

Slowly she used her tongue to trace along the underside of him, then back down one side and up again along the other.

She closed her eyes and pressed her nose against him, breathing in and out with slow deliberation. "Yes."

She took him into her mouth, holding the head of his cock there, not moving. Heat flowed from her, enveloping him, creating sensations that motion and friction could not. He felt her tongue roll over and around him while she continued to hold him there inside her mouth. She opened her eyes. When she pulled back, releasing him and leaving a shiny gleam of saliva, she smiled.

"Can you come more than once, do you think?"

"Yes."

"Would you mind if I taste you? Do it this way the first time?"

He could see that she was squirming, her hips already gyrating slightly as if she were grinding herself on an imaginary cock, even while she looked patiently into his eyes.

"I want to please you," he said.

She bent to him again, more forceful this time, no longer concerned with gentleness, sucking at him strongly as if anxious to receive once again the hot, sticky flavors of a man's sperm on the back of her tongue.

Longarm closed his eyes and let the sensations of her wash through him.

Quickly, much more quickly than usual, he felt the gathering and tightening deep in his loins and then the explosive burst of a powerful orgasm that continued to pump smaller jets of pleasure through him for long seconds afterward.

Jean stayed with him, pressing her lips tight around him and clinging greedily until the last drop was free. When she finally did release him she remained on her knees to milk him with her fingers, using the tip of her tongue to capture the final droplets and savor

108

them. When there was no more, she smiled and sighed. "Thank you," she said.

Longarm took her by the hand and pulled her up onto the bed beside him.

"Lie back now, and close your eyes. No, on the side of the bed just the way you are. That's right."

Very slowly, intent on giving to her the pleasures she had been so long without, he began to explore her body with his tongue. Her throat and ears, breasts and nipples. He licked her belly and the insides of her thighs. She was moaning, thrashing her head from side to side, her hands clenched into fists.

Longarm smiled. He slipped down off the bed and parted her knees so he could get between them.

"You don't have to do that," she said.

"I know." He leaned forward. With his hands he parted the loose, rather prominent lips of her sex and found the tiny red quivering button. She smelled clean and fresh. Gently, slowly at first and then more rapidly, he began to lap at the small button of pleasure with his tongue. He had to press down hard against her stomach to keep her eager, grinding hips under some measure of control. He hoped she would not scream when she climaxed. The neighbors were much too close for that, and her reputation might suffer. But at the moment she did not seem at all concerned about anything like that.

Longarm smiled to himself. By the time he was done here he would be more than ready for another round himself. And they still had a very long night ahead of them.

Chapter 13

Longarm was tired but pleased. It had been closer to daylight than midnight before he finally slipped out of the Briscoe house and headed back to his hotel room, and he had had little time for sleep. But the loss of a few hours' sleep seemed well worth while considering the delightfully hollow sense of satiation that now lay somewhere south of his belt buckle.

He saddled the same gray gelding he had rented before, using his own preferred McClellan instead of the rental stock saddle the livery stable hostler kept insisting came with the price of the horse rental.

He had no idea how long he would be out, following the trail Jean Briscoe had tried to describe for him, and the stores of Gray Rock were not yet open. He had a little jerky in his saddlebags and a few tins of sardines. They would just have to be enough, because he did not feel he should take the time to wait and shop when the store owners found it convenient. The Utes, he knew, would be watching. He might never see them, but someone would be there. They had known when he reached the town. They would know now when he left it. And if it looked like he was dawdling it could only add to the likelihood of a disastrous war to come.

He swung onto the gray's back and let it dance out its early morning reluctance for work. He sat loose and relaxed in the military saddle, letting his weight swing with the horse's choppy jumps and bounces until the animal resigned itself to the inevitable. Then Longarm lined it out on the road toward the Los Pinos Agency.

According to Jean Briscoe, the robbers had taken the public road in a hard, undeviating run until they reached a cutbank where the road dropped sharply. Longarm remembered the spot from his first visit to the agency. Then they had turned west and run under the rim of the cutbank until they reached the Ute burial ground.

It was there, Jean had said, that a group of the Utes had stopped the Gray Rock posse. And somewhere on the other side the Apache police got their licks in at the gang.

Longarm rode slowly, making a show of examining the ground on either side of the wagon-rutted road.

The terrain here was flat and the soil hard-packed. There was little brush or rock where anything, even something as small as a packet of currency, could have been hidden. And had the gang had time to stop and dig a hole with a posse in close pursuit, which they obviously had not, any sign of digging would have been immediately recognizable from a hundred yards away.

Longarm expected to find nothing. But he wanted the watching Utes, wherever they were, to know that he was personally going out and looking for the money. That he was trying his level best to avoid having to violate old Ouray's grave.

To help add to that impression he made it a point to ride out of the road and examine every tuft of sage and every stray rock that looked remotely large enough to conceal something from anyone riding by on the road.

Others quite obviously had done the same thing before him. He found horse tracks, both shod and barefoot, wherever he looked, and he saw an occasional cigar or cigarette butt and once a spoiled handkerchief that some greedy searcher must have dropped.

The many slow side excursions made the ride to the agency far longer than it normally would have been, and he stopped to rest the horse and treat himself to a piece of jerked beef even before he reached the cutbank.

Finally, though, he made it to the point where the robbers had left the road and swung to their right.

He rode along the wall of red rock, formed he knew not how, that was a dozen feet high and extended as far as he could see.

There were more tracks here, some of them possibly left by the robbers themselves and many more added later by the posse and the searchers who had come behind them in ones and twos. After so much passage of time it was impossible for him to separate the tracks and determine which was what.

It did not help that here, in the lee of the cutbank, there was now a solid line of drifted snow left from the brief but vigorous storm of the previous afternoon. Now a good many of the tracks were covered with snow, and if anything had been left along the base of the rock wall it was now buried.

The day was not particularly cold, but still it might be weeks or even longer before the drifts melted. Or it could be next spring, as storms later in the season added to the accumulation. Even if the weather continued as warm as it now was, the drifts would begin to melt but within days the snow would be crusted hard on the surface and would crystallize into spicules of ice that would glaze and resist melting, retaining their cold under a frozen surface in resistance to the sun.

Still, Longarm thought, if there had been anything hidden in so obvious a place, the men who had already looked here would surely have found it already.

Longarm had a new and disturbing thought. *Someone might already have found the money*. They might, for perfectly obvious reasons, be keeping quiet about the discovery. Or they might have left Gray Rock by now, some eighty thousand dollars richer than they ever expected to be.

And if that had happened, unless Longarm could learn about the finder's sudden wealth and recover it, there was no way in the world he could hope to avoid a clash over that gravesite that would surely lead to war between the Utes and the whites.

Thinking about that, and knowing there was no chance he could hope to search this stretch of ground effectively unless he was willing to shovel out several miles of drifted snow, he bumped the gray into a lope and hurried on toward the burial ground.

He had scarcely more than touched spurs to the animal's flank before a spray of stinging gravel geysered up from the ground under the horse's belly, spattering Longarm's boots and the horse's legs and belly with bits of small gravel that felt like birdshot.

A moment later Longarm heard the distinctive report of a distant gunshot.

The rented gray was no Remount Service animal, trained to stand in the face of gunfire. At the first hint of disturbance the gray blew up, leaping into a spasm of bucking that could have unseated a relaxed rider.

As it was, Deputy Marshal Long was not especially

interested in staying on the horse and making an easy target of himself.

By the time the gray reared he was already reaching for his Winchester and throwing himself clear of the saddle. The horse's wild movement only helped him slide free all the quicker, and he hit the ground running.

The shot had come from somewhere on top of the cutbank. There was no way Longarm could scale the wall at this point, not quickly anyway, but he could damn sure get into its protection.

He dashed *toward* the hidden rifleman, under the wall of red stone, wading through snow that was drifted deeper than his knees up close to the wall.

Both sound and distance told him it had to be a man with a rifle out there. If the rifleman wanted another shot at him, he would have to come closer and expose himself to Longarm's return fire to get it.

Longarm cursed a little. He was not going to be that lucky. Not this time. From somewhere at the edge of his ability to hear came the sound of running hoofbeats as the rifleman raced away.

"Bitch," Longarm told himself out loud. He let the hammer of the Winchester down to half cock and wondered if the running horse had been a ruse. Only one way to find out, he told himself. He began looking for handholds for the climb up to the ground level on top of the cutbank.

Longarm was alone on the barren ground, surrounded by nothing but short bunch grasses and odd clumps of gray sage.

After a great deal of searching he was able to find the place the rifleman had fired from. But the only way he was able to tell that for sure was from the empty brass cartridge casing that lay glittering in the sunlight there. The tracks left by man and horse alike were nothing more than unreadable smudges on the hard-baked ground.

He picked the brass up and examined it. A .44-40 case, as common as a flea. Probably half the men within a hundred miles used the .44-40 in both their rifles, and their revolvers. Longarm threw the damn thing aside and began walking back the way he had just come.

He climbed back down to the ground beneath the cutbank only to realize that the untrained livery stable gray was long since out of sight.

It had panicked at the gunshot and the sting of the gravel and might not have stopped running yet.

The damned animal would turn up eventually at the Gray Rock livery, Longarm knew. Unless someone found it and appropriated it first.

But that knowledge hardly solved Longarm's immediate problem of being afoot so far from town.

"Bitch," he said again.

It was closer to the agency buildings from here than it would be to go back to town, but Longarm was not sure of the kind of reception he would get from the Utes until he had had time to fulfill his promise to John Badger. There was also the matter of loss of face to consider if he should walk in there with the admission that a representative of the United States Government had gone and lost his horse.

"Bitch," Longarm muttered. And the hell with them, one and all. The agency was closer. That was where he was going. The damn Utes could think whatever they wanted. He started walking.

His problem was solved, more or less, some ten

minutes later when a young Ute showed up on the horizon leading a spare horse. Longarm stopped and lighted a cheroot and waited for the Indian to reach him.

The Ute reined his own fine-looking Appaloosa pony to a halt a few feet in front of Longarm and held a hand up palm outward. "How," he said in more of a grunt than a word.

The kid's face was impassive, but Longarm was sure he could see the same sort of twinkle in the boy's eyes that he had already learned to recognize in John Badger's.

"Looking for work in front of a cigar store?" Longarm asked him.

The boy—he looked like he was not more than seventeen or so—could not maintain the stonily expressionless set of his face any longer. He grinned.

Longarm grinned back at him. "I thought so."

He accepted the single, jaw-tied rein of the paint horse the boy had been leading and jumped onto the paint's back. The horse wore a handmade Indian saddle of native wood and bullhide that had no stirrups but was surprisingly comfortable once Longarm was on it.

Longarm extended a hand to the kid and shook with him. "I'm Longarm."

"Me, Heavy Balls. Ute brave. Have many coup."

Longarm threw his head back and laughed.

The kid grinned again. "Okay. Charlie Coyote. Not so damn many coup, maybe." He pushed out his hand for a second shake.

"It's a pleasure to meet you, Charlie. You wouldn't happen to be kin to John Badger, would you?"

"Could be."

"I kinda thought so." Longarm balanced the Winchester across the bows of the Indian saddle and offered the boy a cheroot, which he accepted. Longarm lighted it for him. "You just happened to be in the neighborhood?" Longarm asked.

"Something like that." Charlie drew on the cigar without coughing, although it looked like he had to struggle for the first second or two to manage it.

"Yeah, well, I appreciate it."

"Any time." Charlie inspected the glowing tip of the cheroot and offered the impression, "Not bad. Got a drink to go with it?"

"Did have, but I think my saddlebags are halfway back to Gray Rock by now."

"Ugh," Charlie Coyote said.

"Besides which, if I see you take a drink, it's my bounden duty to arrest you and fling your butt into the nearest jail for violating federal law."

Charlie grinned. "Just kidding."

"I believe that. I do."

Charlie reined his rump-spotted horse south, away from the cutbank and away from the burying ground. "Pa says to bring you home now. Unless you want to go back and get that damn gray horse."

"I reckon I can ride along with you. Your pa would be John Badger?"

"Could be."

They rode south, Longarm riding beside the boy instead of falling into single file Indian style. The paint horse did not like it, and Longarm had to keep after him to make the animal respond to the white habit of riding side by side so the riders could talk. Whites rarely gave a damn if some tracker could tell how many there were in a given party.

"I don't suppose you know anything about what's happened to the missing payroll?" Longarm asked.

"Nope."

"Really?"

"Straight talk, Long Arm. I don't."

Longarm nodded. He believed the boy, but it sure would have been easier if the kid had known anything.

"What about the robbers?"

"I got a shot at one. Might've hit him. I think I did." He lowered his voice half an octave and grunted, "Me sing story at council many times, many years. Shoot bad white man. Bang, bang."

Longarm laughed. "I thought it was only your police who were supposed to get in on that action."

Charlie shrugged. "Got to have some fun on the damn reservation. Can't drink. Can't dance. Damn agent shits his pants every time we want to have a dance. Thinks we're gonna take his damn scalp or somethin'." Charlie grinned. "We did think about it, but he's goin' bald. Decided it wasn't worth the trouble."

Longarm laughed again. "Come to think of it," he said, "where is the agent? I haven't seen the man yet."

"You won't," Charlie Coyote said. "Not till this thing is settled. He's either on vacation or at a conference. He never said which. Just left in a big hurry." Charlie laughed. "I think he was makin' up mind pictures about old Meeker staked out with a tent pole through his gut, thinkin' it could happen to him too."

"Could it?"

Charlie shrugged, but this time his face lost the carefree air of happy, zestful youth. The plain truth was that something like that *could* happen again. And John Badger's boy Charlie would probably be right in there helping to drive the pole if it did come to that again.

They rode on in silence after that, and after a polite interval Longarm let the paint have its way about dropping into single file behind Charlie Coyote's horse.

Chapter 14

John Badger was sitting in the dirt outside a solidly built adobe house, leaned up against the mud wall with his derby hat pulled low over his eyes. He looked like he was asleep and he did not look up or seem to notice when Longarm slid down off the paint gelding and thanked Charlie Coyote. The boy took the rein of the paint and rode away leading the animal.

Now that he was here, Longarm thought, perhaps for some reason they did not want him to leave. A hostage? That seemed unlikely. It also might be a bigger job than John Badger figured if that was what they had in mind. Longarm was in no mood today to be anybody's hostage.

"Well?" he asked.

"You are hungry?" Badger still did not look up. He acted like he was still dozing, soaking up the sunshine, which was pleasantly warm with the adobe house cutting off the slight breeze.

"No," Longarm said. "Thank you for the use of the horse."

"You have not found the money."

"No." Longarm decided there was no point in bringing up the matter of the grave again. Not until he had thoroughly checked the route the robbers had taken. Which might well have been John Badger's point in bringing him here.

Longarm hunkered down next to the Ute. No wonder Badger liked the spot, he thought. It was comfortable indeed. He unbuttoned his coat and let it fall open, enjoying the sun for the moment and content to wait for Badger to get around to whatever it was the man intended to say. He pulled out two cheroots and gave one to Badger, then flicked a match aflame and lighted both cigars.

"Nice day," Longarm ventured.

John Badger grunted. As far as Longarm could tell he still had his eyes closed, although he had not hesitated or fumbled when he accepted the smoke.

"The snow came after you said it would," Longarm said.

"The Great One chooses His own time."

"True." Longarm fiddled with his cheroot for a while. "Are you a Methodist too?"

John Badger grunted. The sound could have been taken to mean anything, including that Badger simply did not want to answer.

"Is there anything you want to tell me?"

"Give you," Badger said. "More trouble if you die here. Better if you do not."

"I can agree with that."

Longarm had finished his cheroot and thrown the butt away before Charlie Coyote came riding back, still on his Appaloosa but this time leading a tall, leggy bay gelding that was wearing military issue saddle, blanket, and headstall. The animal was branded with a big US on the left shoulder, indicating that it was, or at least had been, a Remount horse.

It did not take a great deal of imagination for Longarm to realize how the Utes must have acquired a cavalry mount. Last year, about the same time they decided to kill the White River agent and go on the prod, they had also killed a cavalry major and a bunch of his troopers.

"I thought you gave all that stuff back over in Utah," Longarm said. It had been in the mountains of Utah that the reservation jumpers had finally been rounded up, after putting a considerable scare into most of the whites between Missouri and Nevada, and had returned to what was supposed to be a peaceful life at Los Pinos.

"Found this one later," Badger said. "Now we give it back."

"Right." Longarm supposed he ought to believe that. Probably would if he was some kind of wet-eared Eastern boy with a heart that bled easily and often. After all, Injun never speak with forked tongue, and all that crap. On the other hand, any Indian worth his salt was capable of equivocating with the best of them. Longarm guessed that was supposed to be something superior to a plain old lie.

And anyway, it *was* thoughtful of the old boy. The damned livery stable gray had blown up in the face of a little inaccurate gunfire. It could have gotten Longarm into serious trouble. With an army horse that problem would not arise again. John Badger obviously knew that. However thoughtful it was, though, Longarm could not help wondering whether Badger had checked out this particular bay's steadiness under fire . . . say, when he was out in front of some cavalry fire himself a year or so back.

Longarm could not help asking himself that question, but he did not put it to John Badger. He had a hunch he did not really want to know.

"My son will take you back to the trail," John Badger said.

"Thanks." Longarm stood and picked up the Winchester he had leaned up against the front wall of the house.

"Long Arm."

"Yes, John Badger?"

"Better you do not ride into the burying place. Ride around. My son will show you the way."

Longarm thought about that for a moment. He had promised to follow the trail himself, to see for himself. But he was also trying to avoid a war here, and Badger's message was plain enough. His intrusion might be all the hotheads needed to set them off and start the war without a spadeful of earth ever being turned over Ouray's dead and buried body.

"I'll follow Charlie Coyote," Longarm said.

Badger did not answer. His chin sagged down toward his chest, and his breathing became slow and even. He looked for all the world like an aging Indian sleeping in the sunshine, but Longarm did not believe it for a moment. Still, the interview, such as it was, seemed to be over.

Longarm went to the healthy and fully equipped cavalry horse, shoved his Winchester down into a boot intended for a Springfield carbine, and stepped into the saddle.

"Lead on, Macduff."

"Charlie Coyote," the boy corrected.

"Right."

At the slow pace he was forced to take, Longarm needed another day and a half to cover all of the route the robbers had taken, but cover it he did, and thoroughly.

He found a bloodsoaked bandanna one of the wounded men must have dropped. He found enough cigar and cigarette butts to keep twenty men busy smoking at full time for a month or better. And he found a hell of a lot of discarded tin cans and cold campfire coals. But he did not find any trace of the missing money. The searchers had been plenty busy along this trail of late even though the people Longarm ran into—and there were four times as many as he would have expected to see in this empty country—all denied any knowledge of a search for a lost payroll.

Not them. Nosirree, Mister Deputy. They were all out looking for strayed cattle or lost sheep or even—the poor bastard had no imagination at all, Longarm thought—the Lost Dutchman Mine, which was supposed to have gotten misplaced something like four or five hundred miles away. Longarm believed them all. You bet.

Still, they had every right to be there. And as long as they were still out poking alongside of the more and more easily defined trail, they were *not* back at the Los Pinos Agency. That was a definite plus, Longarm decided, so he did not try to discourage any of them. As long as they were out here, they were not back there. And that was something he could be grateful for.

He knew with no doubt whatsoever when he came to the end of the trail.

Buzzards told him that miles before he reached the site.

The actual scene was enough to gag a maggot. There had been no cooling snow down this far south, and the unburied bodies were ripe enough to turn a goat's stomach. What there was left of them, that is. What with the sun and the birds and the foxes and the coyotes, there was not a whole lot left of the men that was recognizable.

And that, Longarm thought, might have been a blessing in disguise since the Apache women had been turned loose on the poor bastards. In their current condition it was impossible to tell what had been done to them.

Even so, incredibly so, Longarm could see boot tracks in the dirt around the bodies indicating that some greedy assholes had been searching even there for any trace of the lost money.

Longarm rode to the end of the trail, took one look, and turned the bay horse back the way he had come.

He had fulfilled his promise to John Badger and, by extension, to the Ute Nation.

Now he had to go back and do his duty to the United States Government.

It was looking more and more, though, like that duty was going to involve the start of a new war between the white and the red people.

Chapter 15

Longarm took the bay wide around the sacred burial grounds. If he absolutely had to start a damned war—and he intended to avoid that if at all possible—it was not going to be over something as foolish as a desire to ride from one place to another in a straight line.

When he got back to the trail he stopped and let the bay rest for a moment. On the way down there had been quite a pack of armed Utes hanging around on the fringes of the burying place, guarding it from intruders. Now there were none in sight. They had to be there, though. Had to be, he thought. He sat on the bay's back and lighted a cheroot. The animal was turning out to be a hell of a good horse; no wonder the Utes had wanted to keep it, with the all-day durability it had given him.

The polite thing to do was to show no interest in where the Indians would be hiding, so he pretended to do nothing more than enjoy his smoke and get down off the bay to take a leak while he searched the rocks and the sage to the west, off toward Ouray's grave and those of many other Utes who had died at Los Pinos.

Finally he spotted some of them. First one and then several others.

A hint of movement gave the first one away when he curled up to scratch his ankle. They were hiding in plain sight, lying out in the open with nothing taller than clumps of dry grass to conceal them.

Once he had seen the first it was less of a trick to find the others. And he was sure there would be more that his roving eye did not spot.

The ones he could see from this place were not wearing white men's clothing, as so many had when he visited the reservation. They were dressed in earth-colored buckskins, and this had thrown him off at first. He wondered if there was some significance to this, and hoped there was not.

Finishing his smoke and his pretended reason for stopping there, Longarm climbed back onto the tall bay and headed back along the trail.

A few miles farther on he reached the western end of the cutbank. Snow still lay drifted along nearly all of its length that he could see, and here and there on the open ground there were still patches of snow built up on the sun-free north sides of objects as small as a healthy sage cluster. It was not obvious while a man rode over the slightly rolling, mostly flat ground, but he must have been gaining elevation ever since he crossed back into Colorado—whenever that had been.

He was not really cold, but riding past so much banked snow made him think that he ought to be, so he buttoned his coat.

As he neared the road, long and prudent habit made him pull the bay down from a ground-eating lope to a slow walk. Always keep your horse fresh enough for a run. It was one of the many things that had become habit with him over the years.

The cavalry horse would be accustomed to the military march pattern of loping most of the time, then being led by a trooper walking beside him with the saddle empty, then a warmup period of trotting under saddle before going back to the swift lope or canter.

It was an effective procedure, so Longarm dismounted again and decided to walk the horse the rest of the way to the road.

He had no sooner gotten on the ground and taken the trailing reins in his right hand when dirt and gravel sprayed underfoot, and he felt his right foot being flung viciously to the right.

The sound of the gunshot came only a heartbeat afterward.

Already off balance, his long legs nearly doing a split when his foot was hit, Longarm moved with the direction the bullet had taken him. He let himself fall and rolled, coming up with his Colt in hand. The Winchester was still booted on the saddle.

At least this time his horse was not panicked. It made no attempt to run, exhibiting no more show of concern than its rapidly flicking ears and a tossing of its head.

Bless the Remount boys, Longarm thought. If he was out here with a foot shot up, he did not want to be without a horse.

He pointed the Colt in the general direction of the top of the cutbank to his north, but he had no target.

Even if he could see someone up there, the would-be assassin would have to be three kinds of damn fool to bring a rifle into pistol range when he had all the advantages.

There was no follow-up shot.

Was the bastard waiting for Longarm to relax? Forget that.

Longarm levered himself upright and hopped wildly on his left foot for the protection once again of that rock wall he had been riding under.

He reached it without hearing another gunshot from above and threw himself into the cushioning snow-drift, his Colt ready.

From afar he heard something that might have been laughter and then the sound of hoofbeats once again.

"Bitch," Longarm murmured. If this was turning into a habit, it was one he could do without.

He rolled over into a sitting position and examined his right foot.

There was no sign of blood, although he was sure he had been hit.

Only the heel of the right boot was missing, torn completely away by the impact of the slug. A slug, he was positive, that would have come from a .44-40 cartridge.

"Bitch," he grumbled again.

He got up and limped back to the waiting bay.

His right foot felt a little numb and was beginning to tingle as the blood flow returned after the sudden shock of the bullet's impact, but otherwise he was unharmed. He still had to walk with an awkward, limping gait because of the missing boot heel.

He gathered the bay's reins and stepped into the saddle. From there he could see onto the top of the cutbank enough to see that there was a rider moving in plain sight up there. He recognized the horse and relaxed.

Charlie Coyote reached the road, came down to Longarm's level, and loped back along the lower side of the cutbank to the waiting deputy.

Longarm gave his face an impassive set, held a hand palm outward, and grunted, "How."

"Ugh," Charlie said with a boyish grin. "People shoot at you a lot?" He reined his Ap to a halt beside Longarm's bay.

"Some." Longarm took two cheroots from his pocket and gave one to the boy. He lighted both of them and said, "Keeps the juices flowing and the appetite up."

"Damn good tobacco you white men bring," Charlie said appreciatively, taking the cheroot from between his teeth and admiring it. "Best reason to let you stay, maybe." He was still smiling. Without any change in tone or expression he added, "My father says maybe you should look for a tall white man with pale hair and Kennedy repeater, eh?"

"Your father says, shit," Longarm told him. "You haven't seen your daddy since I did. Besides, it's a Winchester, not a Kennedy." Kennedy lever action repeaters were mostly sold in the almost equally popular and somewhat more powerful .45-60 cartridge, while Winchesters were .44-40.

Charlie shrugged. "It was far away. Could be a Winchester. Both shaped the same."

"Pretty much," Longarm agreed. He took a deep draw on the cheroot. "Did he see you?"

Charlie Coyote gave him a dirty look. If he had known the expression he probably would have suggested that Longarm go learn to suck eggs.

"By the way," Longarm said, "you should be more careful with your fires. Better yet, learn to do without 'em when you're trying to go on the sneak. The last two nights you've built them where I could see some reflection off the rocks and bushes higher than you."

Charlie gave him another dirty look, but this time the boy looked troubled as well.

"If it makes you feel any better," Longarm said, "I never did catch sight of you or any dust you raised. It was only at night that I could figure out where you were."

The boy tried not to show it, but he was pleased. Longarm suspected he would brag to his father about that tonight and probably forget to mention the fires.

"Tall man with pale hair and lever repeater," Longarm mused.

Charlie nodded.

"What about the horse?"

The boy shrugged. "Brown. No white where I could see. Long way off."

Longarm gave Charlie Coyote another glance. The kid was not particularly tall himself, so his use of that word could mean any damn thing as it applied to a white man. He would probably consider three-quarters of the whites he saw to be tall, while Longarm's opinion of the word would cut that number in half.

And probably half the men in Gray Rock would have pale hair. Blond hair seemed to be common among the people Longarm had seen on the streets, although he had made no particular effort to catalog them by hair color.

So, all in all, Charlie's description of the rifleman would probably apply to fully half of the white men in this corner of the state.

That really narrowed it down, Longarm thought. On the other hand, it was more than he had known. He thanked the kid for the information.

"I'll be going straight on to Gray Rock now," he continued. "Following along the road but not riding in it. You don't have to trail me if you don't want."

Charlie Coyote grinned again. "You won't know which I do, Long Arm."

Longarm laughed. "You're probably right."

They finished their cigars, and Longarm thanked the boy again for the information and told him to say howdy to his dad.

They separated, Longarm turning the bay on the last leg of the ride toward town and Charlie Coyote sitting patient and silent on the Appaloosa behind him.

The kid had been right, too. Longarm never did know for sure if the boy was still trailing along behind somewhere.

Chapter 16

It was evening when Longarm finally reached Gray Rock, but virtually all of the stores were still open and there was an unusually heavy amount of traffic on the streets. Most of the men Longarm saw were on foot, and they were gathered in small clumps and groupings on the street corners and in front of the buildings. Judging from the noise as Longarm rode past, the saloons were doing a brisk and rowdy business.

Longarm howdied the men as he rode by them, but for the most part they looked back at him with what he thought was distaste and few of them spoke.

Odd, he thought.

The liveryman was not on duty when Longarm reached the public stable, so he unsaddled and brushed the bay himself and put the animal into an empty stall. He was pleased but not especially surprised to see that the skittish gray horse was in its accustomed place in the barn. Longarm hung the weather-abused cavalry saddle he had been using on a rack near the bay's stall and looked briefly for his own gear that would have come in on the back of the gray. It was nowhere in sight, though, and he assumed it was locked in the livery office. He could get it in the morning.

Jean Briscoe's town marshal's office was on the way back to the hotel, and there was a light showing through the window so Longarm stopped in.

She was behind her desk, and when Longarm

walked in the front door she gave a glad cry of greeting and ran to meet him, throwing her arms around him and holding him close even though the windows facing the street were uncovered and anyone might have seen them.

"Thank God you're back, Custis."

"I didn't expect *that* much of a welcome," he said.

"You don't know what's been going on here since you left."

"I reckon I don't at that. Would you care to tell me over dinner? I've been giving serious thought to starvation the past couple of days since I managed to get myself left without my own gear."

Jean shuddered. "When that horse came in without you . . . well . . ."

"It didn't mean much."

"Thank God." She hugged him again, then let go of him and began to pace around the room. "Whit Franklin's been shot, Custis." She looked worried.

"And you need me to bring in his killer?" Longarm reached for a cheroot. What he really wanted was a drink, but that could wait a little longer.

"No. You don't understand." She was wringing her hands.

"I reckon I don't," he said with a gentle, slow-down smile. "And I won't, either, until you tell me."

"Whit was shot by the *Indians*, Custis. By the *Utes*."

He scraped a match alight and held it to the tip of his cheroot for a moment before he stuck the cigar in his teeth and began to puff. "I expect that's why there are so many cranky-looking folks on the street?"

"Yes. Everyone is *very* upset."

"Has this Franklin fella been buried yet?" Revenge frequently flared its hottest immediately following a

133

funeral, Longarm knew. If the man had already been buried, there might not be as much of a problem as Jean seemed to fear. If not . . . Well, he was back now. He would handle whatever came as best he could.

"Oh, he wasn't *killed*, Custis. But he was *shot*."

"By the Utes, you said."

"Yes. Shot down right out of his saddle."

Longarm grunted and took a drag at the cigar. He surely did want a drink, almost as bad as he wanted something solid to put a tooth into.

"What does this Mr. Franklin do for a living, Jean?"

"Why?" She acted like she thought he was not giving this anything like a serious enough consideration.

"Curious. Is there some reason you wouldn't want to tell me?" Longarm asked.

"Of course not, but . . ."

"Look, nobody's riding out to slaughter Utes wholesale. Not yet. So, if you don't mind, I'd like to take the time and get this all straight in my head while I can." He smiled and led her to the chair behind her desk, then seated himself at the matching chair in front. "I'm not as smart as some folks, so maybe I have to work at it harder. Okay?"

She smiled and seemed to calm down a little.

"Now, what does ol' Whit do for a living, Jean?"

"He runs a little hardscrabble ranch to the west of town."

"Bachelor?"

She nodded. "Never been married that he's ever talked about, anyway."

"Work the place by himself, does he?"

"Yes."

"No hired hands?"

She shook her head. "He couldn't afford hired men.

134

Even in haying time he has try to put up what he can by himself."

"Uh-huh." Longarm took another drag on the cheroot. "Correct me if I'm wrong, but Mr. Franklin says he was out hunting for strays, minding his own business, and some Indian shot him plumb out of the saddle."

"Exactly," Jean said. She paused for a moment and began to look puzzled. "How did you know?"

"Lucky guess. Where'd they shoot him?"

"At the south end of his place. This is open range around here, but . . ."

"I mean, what part of his body was he shot in?"

"Oh. In the side. High. Almost in the armpit."

"From the front?"

"Yes."

"Did he say from how far away?"

Jean shook her head. "I never thought to ask him that. Is it important?"

"Probably, but I think I already know." Longarm sighed. He damn sure was hungry. "I'm just going to have to stop at the hotel and change out of these busted boots before I get seasick from walking. I'll go put my moccasins on and meet you in the hotel lobby. Then you can take me and we'll have a little talk with Whit Franklin. Meantime, why don't you pin on a badge or something so everybody will know this is an official call and not social, okay?"

"All right."

Longarm went back to his room and got into more comfortable footgear. In the morning he was going to have to hunt up a cobbler. He took the time for a quick nip from the bottle of Maryland rye he carried in his carpetbag and went back downstairs. Jean Briscoe was waiting for him. She had a star-shaped badge pinned over her left breast. Longarm removed his own badge from his wallet and pinned it onto the front of his coat.

There was no hospital in Gray Rock, but the town doctor kept a pair of cots in a room behind his office. Whit Franklin was in one of those. He was surrounded by hard-faced, angry-looking men. Longarm noticed that in addition to the revolvers the men wore strapped at their waists there were a fair number of rifles and carbines piled in a corner as well. Half the long weapons were Winchesters, he noticed in passing.

"Evening, gentlemen," Longarm said.

Jean hurried through a round of introductions, of which Longarm caught probably half and remembered fewer. The men parted and made room beside the bed for their local marshal and the U. S. deputy.

"How are you feeling, Whit?" Longarm asked.

"I hurt bad, Marshal. I swear I do." The man groaned and writhed on the bed.

Longarm could believe easily enough that the fellow was in real pain. Taking a bullet is not pleasant under any circumstances, and where he had been shot the slug had torn layers of large muscles that would shift and move and hurt every time he breathed.

Franklin was bare-chested and swathed in wrappings of bloodstained bandages.

It was not going to be necessary to remove the bandages, Longarm saw. Splotches of dark, dried blood showed clearly enough where the wounds were. He was glad that the visitors were in the room too. That would help get the word around all the quicker.

"Let me help you up for a minute here, Whit," Longarm said.

"What for?" the wounded man asked suspiciously.

"Just want to check something for a second. I'll

just raise you up and lower you right back down. I'll try not to hurt you."

"All right."

Longarm placed a supporting arm behind the man's shoulders, careful not to touch the exit wound at his back, and gently levered him into a sitting position. He shook his head sympathetically and clucked. "Take a look at that, boys. See where that red bastard shot Whit?"

The men automatically crowded close and leaned forward to examine the bloody spot on the back of the bandage wrapping.

"Right there. See it?" Longarm pointed.

The men took a second look and nodded. They had all seen it.

Longarm lowered Franklin carefully back onto the bed. "Hope I didn't hurt you," he said.

"No more'n I could stand."

"Good man." Longarm patted the man's good shoulder. "What was the Injun wearing, Whit?" he asked.

"Huh?"

"The Ute that shot you. What was he wearing?"

Franklin looked puzzled, but he thought for a moment and answered, "Brown pants, I think it was. Dirty. And a blue cavalry coat without no buttons. Yeah, I'm pretty sure that was it." He grinned. "You fixing to go fetch that Injun in an' string the son of a bitch up, Marshal?"

"We'll see. What about the Indian's hat? What kind of a hat was he wearing?"

"Wasn't wearing no hat, Marshal. Had his hair done up in pigtails like them heathen savages wear."

"And his gun?"

"Oh, I seen that real good, Marshal. The sneakin'

red bastard was carryin' a Springfield carbine. Now you *know* where he had to've got one o' *them*. Took it offen the body of some poor dead trooper, he did."

"You were all alone when they ambushed you, weren't you, Whit? Nobody to help. Nobody to fight when they had you down. Isn't that the way it was?" Longarm sounded extremely sorry for the wounded man. "They shot you down when you were out there alone."

"Yeah, that's exactly the way it was, Marshal. I was out lookin' for strays, you see, an'..."

"Marshal Briscoe told me that," Longarm said. "I think we all of us here know how it happened, Whit."

"Damn right. I..."

"Whit Franklin," Longarm said in a sharper tone of voice, "you are under arrest on a charge of violating treaty provisions of the United States government."

"Wha...? I..."

"Shut up, Franklin." Longarm looked at Jean Briscoe. "Marshal, I am placing this prisoner under your custody. I suggest he be allowed to remain here until he can be moved to your jail without injury. I'll arrange for his transportation and trial by a federal court when he is fully recovered from the wounds he suffered while in the commission of his crime."

Neither Longarm's words nor his tone of voice were at all popular in the small room. The men began to shift and mutter. Even Jean Briscoe looked shocked by Longarm's sudden attitude.

Longarm turned to the roomful of men. "Boys," he said, "what we have here is a clear case of Whit Franklin coming damned close to starting a war that would threaten every man here and every woman and child within two hundred miles."

He turned and pointed. "Take another look at those

wounds, boys. A close look this time. Take a look at exactly where those wounds are located."

In spite of themselves, the men looked toward their injured friend.

"He was shot from in front," Longarm said. "The entry wound is a good four inches below the front of his armpit there. Do you see that?"

They nodded.

"We all just looked at where that bullet came out, boys. The exit wound is right smack level with the back of his armpit. Is that right? Do we all remember it that way?"

Again, this time reluctantly, the men nodded.

"Damn right it is," Longarm said. "Think about that. Unless ol' Whit here was laying down on his horse, which I happen to doubt, the only way someone could shoot him at an angle rising that sharp would be if the man with the gun was standing on the ground just a few feet away from Whit's horse."

The men grumbled some, but they had to admit the obvious truth of what Longarm was saying.

"Now nobody, boys, not white nor red nor anything else that I've ever heard of, is going to hide himself *that* good in the kind of country we've got around here. Which means that one of those Ute guards around the grave saw Whit and stopped him from going in and starting a shooting war over that damned missing money."

Longarm took a moment to glare at the men in the small room. "Whit Franklin could have gotten you and me and everyone else around here killed, boys. Because that Ute didn't shoot him down from ambush. The Ute guard came out and talked to him first. I don't know if Whit will ever admit to how it came to shooting, but I can damn well guarantee you that they talked first and then the Ute shot. Probably after good ol' Whit here went for his own gun first."

Longarm looked down at Franklin with a hard glare. The wounded man had a set, stubborn look on his face, but he was not denying any of it either.

"Something else you boys might want to pass around when you get to talking this over. Whit was alone out there. But some damn body got him back here to town where he could get medical help. Who was it?"

Longarm glared around him, as if daring any of them to answer.

"I reckon we all know the answer to that one too, boys. Whit was riding alone out there. Hell, I can't blame him. He was figuring to break the law. Slip in there and steal eighty thousand dollars of the Gray Rock Bank's money. He wasn't wanting to share any of that money with his pals here if he got to it. So when he got himself in a tangle and was on the ground bleeding and needing help, there was only one outfit out there that *could* have brought him in. And that was the same bunch of Ute guards that shot him. Right?"

No one answered. No one was looking Longarm in the eyes now, either.

"What I suggest you boys do now," Longarm said, "is go have yourselves a drink. And while you're at it, I suggest you pass the word along that Whit Franklin is a liar as well as a prisoner of the United States government, and if any single one of you lets this get out of hand, if any *one* of you thinks he's gonna go out there and revenge old Whit, there's going to be hell to pay all through this country, boys. Because right this minute the Utes are out there expecting exactly that kind of trouble. They aren't standing around any longer trying to turn people back from Ouray's grave. They've gone to buckskins and deep holes, boys, and they've got their guns loaded. I saw them myself just this afternoon, and I'm telling you that they are out there expecting exactly the kind of trouble old Whit here damn near stirred up. So *stay away from them*. Leave them be and hope to hell they're willing to do the same, because that's the only hope any one of us has got, boys. *Stay away from those Utes* and pray that I can get this mess worked out before there's real trouble."

Longarm turned and stalked out of the now silent and uneasy room. Jean Briscoe trailed quietly along behind him.

Chapter 17

Longarm tossed his napkin onto the table and shifted his chair a few inches backward. He felt a lot better with his stomach full. The waiter came and refilled his coffee cup. That and a stiff knock of good rye and he would feel like a human again.

"Do you think those boys will pass the word about Whit Franklin and keep everybody away from the Utes?"

Jean nodded. "I think they will. Most of the men around here are family men. They don't want a war any more than you do, Custis."

"Good."

"You look like you feel better."

"Much," he agreed.

"Would you . . . like to come back to my place tonight?"

Longarm smiled at her. *Very* much. Would you mind if I bring a bottle along?"

"Of course not. Burton used to enjoy a drink in the evening too. I miss the taste of it on a man's breath."

"I'll see what I can find at the saloon and join you shortly, then."

"Oh." Jean looked embarrassed. "I almost forgot. Button is at home tonight. But I can send him over to the Robertses for the night. They won't mind, and he will positively adore it. And on your way over, you might stop in at the telegraph office and see if

Wilbur is still there. He tried to deliver a telegram to you the other day and came to me when he couldn't find you in town."

Longarm nodded. "That would be an answer to the questions I sent before I left the other day. How much time do you need before I come over?"

"Half an hour?"

He smiled. "If I can wait that long."

Jean left, and Longarm paid for both meals. He went outside, reminding himself to ask her if there was a good cobbler in Gray Rock where he could get his boots repaired. He felt more than a little conspicuous walking around town in moccasins.

He had no particular desire to return to the Red Garter with its loud noises and gaudy women, so he tried one of the other saloons along the lower end of the street, walking past the bank building on his way down to that end of town.

The bank was long since closed, of course, but he could see a glow of lamplight coming from behind the drawn blinds. Longarm glanced at his watch. It was past eight o'clock. Apparently Cane had had his dinner and returned to the paperwork that he was having to do now without assistance.

The Brass Bass, with an incongruous picture of a fish on its sign in the midst of this dry country, looked like a decent enough place. Longarm went inside.

The trade was brisk here, but Longarm noticed that the men who lined the bar did not look like they were spoiling for a fight now. The word he had put out in the doctor's office must have got around already.

The gaming tables were well attended too, and the women who were waiting on the tables had the cheerful look that said they were making money.

The women in the place were a definite cut above

those he had seen down the street in the Red Garter, although their basic function was almost certainly the same. At least here they were dressed with a measure of decorum, wearing long skirts and frilly blouses and small white lacy caps on their heads.

One of them started toward him with the automatic smile of invitation of her kind, then stopped and took a second look. She turned around and went to talk with another solitary customer.

Longarm was puzzled for a moment until he realized he had forgotten to remove the badge pinned to his coat. He took it off and replaced it in his wallet where he normally preferred to carry the thing.

He found a place at the crowded bar and ordered Maryland rye.

"Got a jug of rye here," the bartender said. "No idea what kind it is. The label come off a while back."

"It will do," Longarm said.

The barman brought the bottle and filled a small glass from it. "Leave it," Longarm said. "I'll carry the leftovers with me when I leave."

"You might want to try it before you say that. Not much call for rye here, so I don't guarantee nothing."

Longarm nodded and tasted the whiskey the bartender had poured for him. It had the smooth, familiar bite to it that he liked. He nodded. "Leave it."

The barman made change from the coin Longarm placed on the bar and went off to serve someone else.

"Assholes an' Easterners drink that horse piss," someone said practically in Longarm's ear.

Longarm turned and gave the man a smile. "Right," he said. "And so do I."

"Yeah, but you're an asshole."

Longarm was still smiling and his voice was calm.

"What is this, neighbor? Been looking for some excitement in your life?" He glanced around the room, confirming what he already suspected. "Is this one of those times when you feel moved to pick out the biggest guy in the room and see if you can take him? I don't mind, actually, but I don't feel like playing just now. So why don't you go bother someone else."

The man—Longarm was sure he had never seen the fellow before—took a half step backward and in a loud voice said, "Looka here. The fuckin' Injun lover loves them red bastards so much he wears their kind o' clothes even." He was pointing down toward Longarm's feet in the beaded moccasins a half-breed Arapaho girl—a very nice girl, actually—had made for him.

The loudmouth had the full attention of the men around them now, and as that attention grew and spread through the bar the big room became silent.

Longarm winked toward the men standing behind the loudmouth and turned back to the bar and his glass of rye. The bartender was standing there again. His hands were out of sight, and Longarm suspected he would have a weapon handy down there.

The tall deputy looked above the bar mirror and nodded toward a brass fish mounted on the wall up there. "Like to fish, do you?"

The bartender blinked, not expecting such an innocuous question. "Uh-huh. I come out here because they said the trout fishin' was awful good. Fella has to make a living too, you know. I close down once a week when the weather's decent an' go up in the hills to fish for trout."

"Good sport," Longarm agreed.

"Yeah."

Behind him, the loudmouth was not willing to let go of it. "See," he declared for all to hear. "No wonder this fed'ral man don't want trouble with the damn Injuns. Top o' lovin' them, he's yellow." The man cackled, and there was a stir of discontent among the crowd.

Longarm sighed and turned back to face the man. Over his shoulder he told the bartender, "This is commencing to become official, friend. Better you should stay out of it."

The barman nodded and reached under his bar. Longarm could hear wood against hard wood as he laid something down there out of sight. At least this time Longarm would not have to worry about interference from behind.

"Now," Longarm said to the bigmouth, "what is it I can do for you, neighbor? Besides cart you off to jail on a charge of fucking with the wrong officer, that is?" He was smiling again, but probably no one in the room was dumb enough to take that seriously.

Longarm looked the loudmouth over. The man wore corduroy trousers and tall, lace-up boots. Longarm thought he might have been a freighter or some other such transient who could skip out of the country laughing if the Utes went to war against those whose homes and families were lodged here.

The man did look fit enough, thick-bodied but hard and with a heavy pad of muscle on his shoulders that gave the impression that he had no neck. His nose looked like it had been broken many times in the past, and there was a prominent buildup of scar tissue over his eyes. He wore a full beard, but Longarm suspected there would be plenty of scars hidden under the blond growth.

Longarm looked at the man again. The fellow was a good four inches shorter than the officer he faced. But that might easily be tall enough for Charlie Coyote to call him tall. The kid had not mentioned a beard, but the hair color certainly fit.

"Yellow," the man repeated. He looked around to the others in the room for encouragement, although none of them looked half as belligerent as this fellow seemed to feel.

"I told you once, neighbor. I don't feel like playing right now." Longarm's voice was still mild, but his eyes were like gunmetal ball bearings.

The man might have been in many fights, but apparently he was not smart enough to have learned a whole hell of a lot from them. When he decided to throw the first punch, he telegraphed the fact as clearly as if he had had bright red signal flags in his fists. He drew back, took slow aim, and let one fly.

Longarm felt almost disappointed. He stepped lightly to the side and let the stocky fighter throw himself forward against the polished wood of the bar.

Longarm banged a series of swift, vicious jabs into the man's kidneys and stepped back before the fellow ever had time to turn around.

When he did he came around swinging, a wild, looping right that would have taken Longarm's head off his shoulders if he had been dumb enough to stand and wait for it. But by that time Longarm had shuffled sideways and was once again behind the man, pummeling his kidneys.

The man roared and whirled, again with a wild swing that came nowhere near its intended target.

"Slow to figure things out, aren't you?" Longarm asked. He raised his arms in a Marquis of Queensbury stance and flicked his forearms up and out in time to the loudmouth's punches. Each intended blow was picked out of the air and diverted harmlessly aside.

If this kept up, Longarm decided, he was going to end up with bruises and sore arms. He deflected an overhand right and jabbed with his own left, connecting twice with his left and following with a right that went straight from his shoulder to the point of the loudmouth's chin.

The man's lips pulped, and blood flew when the idiot shook his head like a cornered, gutshot buffalo bull.

"Give it up," Longarm suggested. "I'm not quite as yellow as you'd like to think. And you *damn* sure aren't half as tough as you want people to believe."

The man responded with a kick aimed at Longarm's crotch. It was not a sensible decision for him to have made.

Longarm twisted his knee up and to the side and took the kick on his thigh. He was mad now. He gave serious consideration to saying the hell with fair play and stomping this son of a bitch into the floor, and he might have done exactly that except that he was not wearing his boots.

Instead, angry, he extended his knuckles and jabbed the man hard in the throat.

The man went pale and clutched at his throat with both hands.

With no defense to worry about at all now, Longarm drove a wickedly hard right deep into the pit of the man's gut, and when the fellow doubled over Longarm kneed him in the face.

The barroom brawler flipped over onto his back and curled himself in a tight ball of agony, not sure of where he should try to grab and comfort himself first.

Disgusted with himself, with the man lying on the floor, and with every man in the place, Longarm picked up the crockery jug of rye whiskey he had paid for and stomped out of the Brass Bass.

Chapter 18

Longarm rolled her nipple between his lips, sucking gently at her breast, and Jean moaned and arched her back toward him. Twice already his lips and tongue and knowing fingertips had brought her to shuddering, groaning climax, and he could feel that she would soon be ready again.

She opened her eyes and smiled at him in the moonlight that was streaming through the bedroom window. She looked good in this light, he thought. When she was just a few years younger she must have been one hell of a fine-looking woman. For that matter, he reflected, she was quite all right just as she was.

"Now," she whispered. "Please."

She reached for him, her fingers finding and caressing him, guiding him over her belly and down into the hot, ready wetness of her eager flesh.

He lowered himself onto her, filling her. She took in a deep, quick breath of intense pleasure and craned her neck to reach his mouth. He kissed her, enjoying the feel of her tongue inside his mouth, enjoying even more the heat that engulfed him further down.

"Take me," she said. "Hard."

He began to move.

"Harder. You can't hurt me." She smiled. "Try, Custis. Try to hurt me with your belly." She laughed and raised her legs, opening herself to him fully, spreading herself wide for him and clutching him fiercely around the waist.

"I don't want..."

"Please. It's all right, Custis. You won't hurt me."

He did as she asked, drawing back until he nearly slipped free from her, then plunging forward onto the yielding softness of her stomach.

He could feel her pelvic bones, sharp and fragile under their clothing of living flesh, dig into him, and Jean gasped.

Apologetic now, he stopped. "I knew I'd hurt you."

She laughed again and shook her head happily from side to side. Her long hair, unpinned and falling loose now, flowed softly against the pillow. "You didn't," she said. "Honestly. Don't stop now. It's perfect."

"All right."

Reluctantly at first, then with a growing need of his own, he withdrew and lunged forward, withdrew and plunged.

He was still afraid that he might be hurting her, but Jean bit her underlip and raised herself to meet him with hips that were thrusting as wildly as his were. No, he realized, he was not hurting her. She was enjoying the feelings every bit as much as he was.

He could feel the gathering flow now but he did not want to come before she was ready.

He slowed just a little, and Jean changed her pace to match his.

She took a deep, ragged breath, and her fingernails dug into his back. She must have remembered the open window nearby, because she was struggling against a desire to cry out. Instead she was making small, mewling noises deep in her throat, and her hips became more insistent, picking up the rhythm and taking him along with her as she brought the pace once again up toward frenzy.

"Uhh-ngh-guh-uh-uh-uh!" She sounded like she was

choking on something, trying to hold back the sounds, but her body betrayed what was really happening. She dug her nails into him all the harder, and her legs quivered and scissored tight around his hips as Longarm let himself tip over the brink of sensation and pump his fluids with explosive force deep inside her.

Longarm clenched his teeth and arched his back, the cords of sinew and muscle standing out along the line of his neck as the pleasure reached an almost unbearable level and finally, mercifully, subsided.

Jean continued to hold him, kept her arms and her long legs wrapped tight around him. She pulled him down on top of her overheated body, cushioning him on her breasts, taking all of his weight onto herself. She was still making small, glad sounds deep in her throat.

"Are you crying?"

"No," she said. She reached around his shoulder and wiped a shiny tear from the corner of her eye.

"Then what was that, ma'am?"

"Joy." She was smiling.

He kissed her eyes, first one and then the other. "I was afraid I'd hurt you."

"Never," she said. "Not like that. You can only please me that way, Custis. Please me greatly." She sighed and wriggled, pushing at him now.

He let her roll him off her satisfied form and he lay on his back. He reached higher on the bed to find a pillow and pull it down under his neck.

"Would you like a smoke now? Or a drink?"

"One of each would be nice."

Apparently more than willing to wait on him, Jean left the rumpled bed and walked naked in the moonlight to find first a glass and the bottle, then his cheroots and matches. She brought them back to him and lighted the cigar for him, then poured a generous tot of rye.

She sat on the edge of the bed, and he admired the fullness of her breasts and the flat, smooth planes of her stomach. "You should never wear clothes when the moon is up," he told her.

Jean laughed. She sounded pleased, though. "If that is true, sir, then *you* should never wear clothes at all." She reached out to fondle him. "I hope this comes back to life again."

"I suspect it will, ma'am. Just give it a little time and it'll be good as new."

"Good." She bent briefly to kiss him there, then sat up again with a smile and licked her lips.

Longarm chuckled. "Very little time, I'd say."

"All the better then, sir." She bent and found a soiled undergarment on the floor, one of her own, and used the cloth to wipe herself. "You're a very messy fellow, did you know that?"

"I can keep it to myself if you'd like."

"Don't!" she cried with mock horror.

Longarm shrugged and took a swallow of the rye. "Whatever you wish, ma'am."

"You *know* what I wish." She left his side and came around to crawl back onto the bed next to him. She nestled her head against his shoulder and smiled at him while he finished his cigar and enjoyed the rest of the drink.

When he was done she sighed. "I suppose I really ought to feel quite shame-filled and guilty about this."

"But you don't."

"No, I truly do not." She sighed again. "The truth is, sir, I haven't felt this good since . . . since Burton died."

Longarm turned his head and kissed her on the tip

of her nose. "You are a good woman, Marshal Briscoe. Too fine a woman to be alone. The man who ends up marrying you will be one lucky fellow indeed. In a lot of ways, ma'am, I wish it was going to be me. And whether you know it or not, that is one mighty high compliment indeed."

She smiled and ran a hand over his chest. "I do know it. But you aren't the marrying kind. Won't be as long as you are doing the work you do. I understand that, Custis. While you're here, though—" she poked him in the ribs, hard—"I intend to get all that I can out of you."

"Good for you," he said. "That's an attitude a man can get along with."

She laughed.

He lay back and enjoyed the feel of her warmth next to him. From out of nowhere a thought came to him as he remembered passing the bank with the light still burning inside—much more enjoyable to be in bed like this than seated alone in a cold office—and he asked, "Tell me about Sam Cane."

"Are you serious?"

"Uh-huh."

"If you insist. Let me see now, P. Samuel Cane."

"P?"

"It stands for Pearl. Sam *hates* that name. It's a well known fact in Gray Rock that anyone who calls Sam by his first name will never get another loan from the bank here. Or from any other bank, if Sam hears about it first. What else?" She hesitated while she thought. "He is married to Marilyn Hardifer Cane," she said.

"Hardifer?" Longarm asked. "Isn't that the name of the bank president who was killed during the robbery?"

"Yes. Walker was Marilyn's older brother."

"Was Cane a banker before he married, or did that come afterward? Keeping it in the family, so to speak?"

"I really don't know, Custis. Is it important?"

"I doubt it. Just a question."

"Well, they came here together. After the Halleluia was opened, and the town got big enough so you'd notice it if you happened to be riding through. Before the mine was discovered, there really wasn't much to Gray Rock. Burton and I were already here, of course. The Hardifers and the Canes came later."

"What do you know about the Hardifers?" he asked.

"Not very much. Walker seemed to consider himself above the rest of us. At least, he certainly did not socialize here. I don't know what he was like elsewhere, of course. He did like to get away now and then. At least twice a year he would go to conventions in Denver or Kansas City or some such place."

"Did his wife go with him when he traveled?"

"Oh, Walker never married." Jean laughed. "Everyone around here said he was too cheap to marry. Couldn't stand the thought of putting out money for a ring. And when he did travel, he always made it clear that he was going in the interests of the bank and the depositors. Of course that was so the bank would pay for his travel. I don't think the poor man ever understood that we all knew that. Not that we minded. Walker always paid good interest on deposits. Two percent without fail. We could always count on that."

"Good manager, then," Longarm said.

"Oh, yes. Walker was as careful with our money as he was with his own." She laughed again. "I really think the poor thing regarded money as . . . holy, almost."

155

Longarm nodded. "I've known a lot like that. Never really understood it myself, but I've sure known a lot who feel that way."

"Exactly." Jean leaned down and bit his shoulder, nipping his skin between her teeth hard enough that it hurt.

"Hey!"

"Are we going to talk all night, or what?" she asked.

"What'd you have in mind?"

"Well . . . if you aren't too old to get it up again . . ."

He reached down and spanked her bottom with his open palm. Judging from the most satisfactory sound he produced, it must have stung more than he intended.

"Ouch!" Jean complained.

"I'm still waiting to hear what you had in mind, lady."

Jean smiled at him.

"If I was a bad guy, Marshal," he said, "I'd sure worry if you smiled at me like that."

"Ho ho, Deputy. It is my intention to place you under my complete and total control."

"Really, now. And how do you propose to do this foul deed?"

"Wait and see, buster. Just you wait and see."

Still smiling, she bent over him. "Hands at your sides, Deputy. And don't you *dare* move."

Longarm went along with her, although he had no idea what she was up to. He put his hands down at his sides and lay still.

"Bet you can't stay still now," she said.

"Bet I can."

With a giggle Jean bent lower. She leaned forward

156

until her hair was falling free over her breasts.

Softly, barely touching him, she began to weave her upper body back and forth over him, the tip ends of her hair barely touching and teasing him.

The whisper-soft touch ranged across his stomach and then lower, tantalizing the rising shaft of his manhood and dropping down to tickle his balls.

"I knew you'd move," Jean said, looking at his cock.

"No fair," he protested.

"All right. That isn't the only thing I can get to move."

"Of course it is, woman. I have a well-known will of solid iron."

"Hah!" She tossed her head, throwing the cascade of dark, gleaming hair back over her shoulders, then bent low again.

The tip of her tongue flicked out, teasing and arousing him. Licking and darting, touching here and swirling there.

"You fight dirty, you know that?"

"Uh-huh." She stopped what she was doing and looked at him, her eyes alight with laughter. "You realize, of course, that I am not going to stop doing *this*, or do a single thing *more*, until you put me where you want me. Anyplace at all. That choice is up to you, dear Custis. But I don't do *anything* else until you reach out and move me. In which case I will have won."

She laughed, and her tongue flickered and quivered busily at its task.

"This isn't going to work, woman," he threatened.

"Of course it is." She went back to what she had been doing.

Longarm groaned. Then he started to laugh. After all, a wise man always knew when he met defeat. He reached for her.

At the moment, though, Jean was much too busy to take time out for gloating. She could do that later. While he rested.

Chapter 19

Longarm left the widow Briscoe's house well before daylight to avoid causing problems for her in the small town. After breakfast alone in the hotel, he found the cobbler and saddlemaker's shop and left his boots there for repair. The man said it would take several days to replace the heel, although he certainly did not look so busy that it should take so long. Still, it was the only place in town where the work could be done.

Then, finally, he got around to stopping in at the telegraph office for the message Jean had said was waiting for him there.

He accepted the flimsy sheet of paper and signed for it. When he read the answer to his request he was almost disappointed.

"I hope you know how to keep your mouth hushed about private matters," he told the operator.

The man nodded. "Lots of practice," he said.

Longarm walked on down to the marshal's office, where Jean Briscoe was at work behind her desk. He sat wearily in the chair nearby and tossed the telegraph form in front of her.

"What is this?" she asked.

Longarm shrugged. "A long shot that didn't pay off," he said. "I was thinking that just maybe Jerry Peak managed to give himself a bonus. Thought maybe the man wasn't doing as well as he likes to say, you see."

"And of course Jerry would know all about the

159

cash in the vault since it was intended for his mine, and he would know that the insurance company would make the loss good if it was stolen before he picked it up that afternoon."

Longarm nodded. "He was a bit late getting to the bank that afternoon. If he and his guards had already been inside when the robbers showed up, there likely wouldn't have been any robbery."

"It's pretty normal for them to be late," Jean said.

"And judging from that telegraph there, Jerry Peak doesn't need to steal from anybody. Like I said, it was a long shot, and like most of those it didn't pay out."

Jean picked the form up from the desk, read it, and let out a slow, low whistle. "I assumed Jerry was doing well with the mine. But *this* well?"

Longarm laughed. "Apparently having a gold mine of your own is everything folks say it is. Good as gold. And this is just from the man's personal accounts. They say if I want the corporate account figures they'll have to get them separate."

Jean shook her head with awe. Jerry Peak's personal bank accounts held cash assets of more than four hundred thousand dollars. The happy, hard-working miner had no reason to steal from himself, Longarm thought. He already as good as owned the keys to the Denver mint.

"Pity he's already married," Longarm said. "I'd sure give you a good recommendation."

Jean lowered her eyes and blushed. Apparently now, in the light of day, she was uncomfortable discussing or even remembering the bold demands she had made of him through a long and satisfying night.

"What will you do now?" she asked, changing the subject quickly.

"Not much I can do now," he said, "except go out to the agency and hope I can talk John Badger and his friends into opening that grave. It's the only thing left to do, and we all know that sooner or later that grave is *going* to be disturbed, with or without their cooperation."

He pulled a cheroot from his pocket and bit the tip off with more anger than care, spitting the leftover scrap of tobacco out without thinking. He lighted the cigar, his gloomy mood obvious on his tanned face.

"Damn it, Jean," he said, "I don't like this, but I don't know what else I can do. That order is already written and in my pocket. I've delayed just about all I can in executing the thing. I'm afraid if the Utes won't voluntarily let me open Ouray's grave, I'm gonna have to do it anyway."

"If it comes to that, Custis, please bring in the army to back you up out there."

He sighed. "That won't eliminate the problem, you know, just postpone it. The troopers could be there to protect me while I open the grave, but they won't be able to protect every man and woman that lives in this country. No way they could manage that if the Utes really decide to put on paint and jump the reservation again."

"I know."

"Damn it," Longarm muttered again, "there just isn't any other way."

John Badger seemed determined to avoid discussion of the problem that had brought Longarm here. He and the other elders of the Ute nation spoke at long and flowery length about nearly every other topic under the broad, blue sky. But not a word was mentioned about Ouray or graves or missing money.

Two things, though, told Longarm that the men were all damned well aware of the seriousness of this discussion: once again every woman and youngster in the neighborhood seemed to have miraculously disappeared; and nearly all of the men—absolutely all of the younger Utes—wore traditional buckskin britches instead of the more comfortable white man's cloth. The men were not wearing paint. Not yet. But they were damn sure ready to throw off their coats and daub on the paints.

Even John Badger wore fringed buckskins beneath his filthy coat and derby hat. Longarm regarded that as possibly the worst sign of all. John Badger was definitely emerging as a strong leader among his people now that Ouray was gone. And John Badger was ready to go to war over the sanctity of the dead chief's grave, regardless of the words he was willing to speak now. The simple change of clothing signaled that as powerfully as a war cry could have done.

"Your people are generous," Longarm said, accepting another cup of the homemade *tizwin* from Charlie Coyote. The fermented horse piss—at least that was what it tasted like—was entirely illegal on the government reservation, of course, but this would not be a good time for Longarm to remember that.

In return Longarm passed around another handful of cheroots. He had bought several boxes of them in Gray Rock before he left for Los Pinos and charged them to Uncle's expense account. This was not a full ceremonial occasion when the use of the ancient medicine pipe would be called for, but a little friendly smoking never hurt.

"You have been away," Badger said. It was as close as he had yet come to mentioning the reason for

162

Longarm's visit. "The man called Long Arm tries to help his friends the Utes."

Longarm wanted to speak, but Badger was rambling on. "The man called Long Arm rides far to keep his promises and does not blame his friends when a bullet seeks him from hidden places."

"My friends are men," Longarm said. "Men do not hide in the sage and lurk behind rocks to shoot. You are my friends. You are strong and you are men. If I offend you, you will come to me and stand before me with your gun in your hand, as I will have a gun in my hand. But that is not what friends wish for each other."

"This is true," Badger said, "but friends are also courteous."

Longarm had no idea what John Badger was trying to tell him. He waited.

Badger sat for a time sucking on the cheroot Longarm had given him. If Longarm did not know better he might have thought the impassive Ute had drifted away from the conversation at hand.

"True friends have respect for the widows and orphans of their friends and of their enemies," Badger said after a time.

Longarm nodded, but he still had no idea what in hell John Badger was getting at.

"Does Long Arm have respect for the widow of the Arrow?" Badger asked.

"Of course."

"Long Arm has not shown this."

"Long Arm has not seen this good woman who might have been his grandmother. Long Arm has great respect for Chipeta," Longarm said formally. Inwardly he was wondering why in the *hell* John Badger was messing around with all the side issues today. Hell, on the other side of the camp the youngsters were probably already loading and cleaning their rifles and putting a fresh edge on their knives. Yet Badger and the others were gathered around with their fingers up their noses. Longarm was beginning to wonder if they were up to something specific. He hoped they were not, but he wasn't going to count on anything.

Badger turned and beckoned his son closer. The two whispered together for a moment, and Longarm caught a hint of an English word. Badger paused for a moment and repeated it back to his son, and Charlie Coyote corrected him. Badger nodded. He turned back to Longarm.

"Our grandmother has been in mourning," Badger said. He hesitated. "Do I say this correctly?"

Longarm nodded.

"Yes, our grandmother has been in mourning. It has not been permitted to disturb her prayers to the great white God. Now she is returned to her people. It is in our minds to think that the man called Long Arm should tell his grandmother of his sorrow at the Arrow's passing."

Damn, Longarm thought. *Another delay*. He was convinced by now that the Utes were delaying on purpose here, getting ready for a breakout possibly, stalling him while they made their preparations.

But if he failed to go along with them in the stall and forced the issue now, he would only be setting the time for the outbreak. He still wanted to prevent it instead.

"Long Arm would like to tell his grandmother Chipeta of his true sorrow," he said courteously.

Without a word to the other Utes gathered in the circle, John Badger stood and began walking away

164

from the fire. Longarm hesitated for a moment, not sure if he should follow, then stood and hurried to catch up with the Ute.

They walked together but in silence toward the frame bungalow the federal government had built for Ouray as part of its deal with the old chief when last year's outbreak was finally ended.

The house was painted white and tidy-looking, although already the effects of heat and cold and wind had begun to blister the paint, trying with slow and indomitable strength to return the lumber to dust. Soon the house would need maintenance. Longarm wondered if the Utes would know how to do it, or if the agent would care enough to tell them.

John Badger opened the gate in the low picket fence that surrounded the house, both bungalow and fence seeming so far out of place here in this sere, rust-colored land. The Ute carefully closed and latched the gate behind them.

The Indian did not speak to announce their presence when they reached the open front door, so Longarm assumed that they were expected. People who spend much of their lives in skin tents are uncommonly respectful of one another's privacy.

Inside, the little house was furnished with a curious mixture of articles from two separate worlds. There were plush chairs and an ottoman covered with heavy velveteen or some such substance, but at some point after the manufacture of the white-style furnishings the owners had added painted symbols and horsehair decorations and a great many ermine tails.

Beside a carved and gilded Louis XIV chair there was a backrest woven from green willow and an old, much-decorated parfleche for storage.

The floor was covered with a thick layer of buffalo

165

robes. The robes had been brought down from the mountains or even from the plains far to the east, because there were no buffalo in this country and never had been.

Ouray's widow sat in an overstuffed armchair. She was tiny and the chair was huge, and at first Longarm had not seen her there among the mementoes of her long life.

He took his hat off and approached her. "My greetings to you, little grandmother," he said. "My heart is full of sorrow at your loss."

She smiled at him. At least he thought she did. The wrinkles and folds around her toothless mouth shifted position, anyway. She nodded her acceptance of his sympathy.

From where she sat, lost in the depths of the chair, she seemed almost enthroned there. She said something in her own language and motioned toward the floor at her feet. John Badger sat crosslegged in front of her, and Longarm took the hint and did the same.

She began to speak, very slowly and in the Ute tongue, and Badger translated for her. Longarm was almost sure that he remembered Chipeta speaking at least some English, but either he misremembered that or she was simply choosing not to use the foreign language.

At some length she told Longarm that she remembered him well, that she was pleased to see him again, that he was a great man and a friend to all the Ute people, that she appreciated his sorrow, and more.

While she talked and John Badger repeated her words in slow English, Longarm had a better chance to look at her.

The last time he had seen her she had had all her fingers. Now she was missing the little and third fingers on both hands, the fingers chopped off neatly at the second joints. The wounds were still scabbed over, so they were relatively new.

If Chipeta had been in mourning, Longarm thought, she must have found a new wrinkle to Methodist practices.

For that matter, he hadn't thought that the Utes practiced that particular mourning habit. He was not sure about that or even whether Chipeta might once have come from another tribe with other customs. It could well be that in her grief she had reverted to the customs of her childhood. Whatever the reason, she for damn sure had been serious about her mourning. It would take a ferociously strong will for a person to lop his or her own fingers off.

Chipeta continued to rattle on, with Badger droning along behind her in English. Longarm was barely paying attention at this point. He was giving much more of his actual attention to a tight-stretched and age-dried skin drum hanging on the wall behind the little crone. He was vaguely aware that she was telling him about her mourning.

"All this time," Badger was saying, "your grandmother had no tent, no blanket. She slept on the ground with a rock for a pillow and the call of the coyotes for a song. She sang the death chants through each long night and ate no food and drank no water but the little she had taken with her. She did as her people have always done since the beginning of time and offered up prayers to the great white God also, as the Arrow would have wished her to do. In all this time no human person has been permitted to approach or disturb her. In all this time she has listened only to the voices of the birds in the air, who spoke to her of the high place where the Arrow now rides, and the

167

voice of the coyote who told her of the path she must take when she follows the Arrow to the high place on the other side. Our grandmother did these things until in the night a coyote came to her and whispered into her ear that she should now return to her people, and a rabbit came to her and gave our grandmother its meat so she would have the strength to walk back to her people and join us, to listen when we sing about the deeds of the Arrow, and to take her place as our honored grandmother once again."

Longarm was listening intently now. Even when Chipeta, by way of John Badger, recited a long, long list of Ouray's accomplishments and his battles.

Finally the old woman shut up. And when she was done, she was damn sure done. She closed her eyes and leaned her head back against the upholstery of the huge chair, and as far as Longarm could tell she was sound asleep. She didn't so much as twitch when Longarm and John Badger stood and left the house.

"You will go now?" Badger asked as they walked back toward the fire.

"Yes," Longarm said.

"What shall I tell the young men who wish to fight?"

"Tell them that the time is not now. With luck, John Badger, who could have been my brother if my skin was dark, the time for fighting will not come again."

Badger nodded.

"Don't pull your guards off for a couple days, though," Longarm said. "It will take a little while for the word to get around that I've recovered the missing money."

Badger nodded again. "When it is done," he said, "my brother Long Arm should come once again to visit his friends. We would drink much, my brother and me. We would eat fat meat and spend the nights with warm, fat girls, eh?" Badger chuckled.

"It sounds good," Longarm said. "We can ride together to hunt the fat meat, and in our camp at night we can laugh with the fat, warm girls."

"I will bring my son on this hunt. And a daughter to share my brother's bed. You have sons?"

Longarm shook his head. "Reckon I'm not as lucky that way as my brother."

"I am sad for you, Long Arm." John Badger grinned. "You try hard. With luck you may have a son in the summer to come."

"I'll try hard," Longarm promised.

They reached Longarm's horse and shook hands. "Tell the rest of my friends here that I would like to feast and drink with them tonight, but first I have to go get that money back for the bank." He mounted and headed for town, feeling better than he had since Billy Vail gave him this assignment.

Chapter 20

It was nearly dark when Longarm got back to Gray
Rock. The number of people on the street, many of
them drifting toward the saloons, told him that the
work shift at the Halleluia had shut down. He saw
Ralph, the clerk in Jerry Peak's office, and spoke to
the man.

"How's it going, Marshal?"

"Just fine now, Ralph. You?"

"Couldn't ask for better."

"Me neither." Longarm rode on. He came abreast
of the bank building and saw a light behind the drawn
blinds. Sam Cane was working late again, although
it would soon be time for him to hurry home for his
supper.

Longarm thought about going on to the marshal's
office and seeing Jean first. After all, this was her
town and her worry. But there would be time enough
for that later. And he wanted to talk to Cane about
the missing money. If he went to see Marshal Briscoe
first—Longarm was having more and more difficulty
thinking of her that way—he would probably miss
Cane and have to go to look for the man at his home.
Better to talk to him now. He reined the horse over
to a hitching post in front of the bank building and
dismounted.

A miner came by on the sidewalk. Longarm thought
he recognized the man from his visit to the mine, but

either he had never heard the man's name or he could not now remember it.

"Are the Utes gonna break out, Marshal?" the man asked.

Longarm smiled and shook his head. "No, and there's no need for anybody to go digging up Ouray's grave now either. I've found the missing money."

"Yeah? Where?" The man grinned. "I got to admit I did some looking my own self on my day off. Where was it?"

"I'll put the word out later. Meantime, it wouldn't hurt any if you'd pass it along that everything is gonna be okay now."

"You bet." The miner's grin got broader. "Hell, Marshal, with news like this, I'll bet I can work up a skinful o' free drinks at the Garter."

Longarm laughed, and the miner hurried on down the street. Longarm could see him stopping and talking excitedly with everyone he met. Good enough. In no time at all, all of Gray Rock would have heard the news.

Longarm knocked loudly on the door of the Gray Rock Bank. He got no response at first, so he hollered through the glass, "Open up, Sam! I have some news for you. This is Deputy Long, Cane. Open up."

Cane came to the door. He opened it, but he did not look pleased with the interruption. He let Longarm inside and carefully locked the door behind him and tugged against it to satisfy himself that the deadbolt was fully seated.

"What is it you want now, Marshal? I'm very busy, you know. I haven't time for these constant visits of yours." It was the second time Longarm had ever set foot in the bank.

"Official business," Longarm said. Without waiting for an invitation, he walked into the back of the bank and past the tellers' windows to the office portion of the building.

He stopped just inside the windows. "I didn't know you had company." Longarm grinned. "But I reckon this saves me from having to go out and look for you," he said to the other man in the office.

The man gave him a cold stare.

Longarm looked him over. The man was past middle age, approaching a point of becoming elderly. He was tall and extremely thin and wore an immaculately clean business suit, crisp collar, and carefully knotted tie. His hair was snowy white and looked like the gentleman washed it at least once each day. He was clean-shaven and pink-cheeked even at this early evening hour; probably he had freshly shaved before he left the hotel. Longarm was certain he would be registered at the hotel. He had the quiet, distinguished bearing of another banker come to do business here.

"Jonas Hightower, right?" Longarm said.

The man's expression did not change, but his eyes hardened.

"I've read about you," Longarm went on. "Paperwork out of Ogden and all that. They say you're a real expert."

Hightower coughed, but his hands remained motionless and relaxed in his lap. He made no move to cover his mouth when he coughed, nor did he speak.

"Yeah, a real expert," Longarm said.

With his left hand, Longarm reached into a hip pocket and pulled out a pair of handcuffs. He tossed them onto Cane's desk in front of Hightower.

"You can save us both a lot of trouble if you'd put these on without a fuss," Longarm said. "And in case you're worried about it, you won't take a long fall.

172

I'm more'n willing to testify that you weren't shooting at me exactly. If you had been, I reckon I'd be dead now."

Hightower seemed to be considering it. The set of his facial muscles relaxed. Longarm had not even noticed how much tension the man had been under, but now the difference was remarkable.

"Thank you," Hightower said.

"Of course I'd also want your corroborating testimony about Sam here hiring you to try and scare me off."

"I told him it wouldn't work," Hightower explained. "But he was afraid of a federal investigation if you were killed here."

"Actually, he was right about that," Longarm said. "I expect you were both right. Except for starting all this in the first place."

"You know, of course, that I had nothing to do with the initial...uh...difficulty."

"I figured that out. Sam brought you in later for protection."

"I told him to either kill you or run. You are not the kind to be frightened away by a few gunshots. And my fee, frankly, would have been the same regardless. My services are not discounted." The Mormon assassin spoke with dignity and no small degree of pride.

"You have a high reputation for your field," Longarm said.

Hightower nodded. He looked almost regal doing it, accepting the praise and honors that he considered his due.

Well, Longarm thought, he was entitled, in a way. Jonas Hightower was as fine a marksman as ever fired the Creedmore long-range target series. And about as accomplished a killer for hire as had come down the pike in a long, long while.

"I was particularly pleased with the shot at your boot heel," Hightower said.

"That was really deliberate?"

Hightower nodded. He looked genuinely pleased with himself.

"Fine shooting," Longarm admitted. He smiled. "But I might have to throw into our little agreement here that you pay for the repair to that boot."

It was Hightower's turn to smile. "You tempt me, Long, but surely you understand that a man my age could not enjoy the rigors of involuntary confinement."

"And surely you understand, sir, that your choices are limited. As excellent as you are with a rifle—and I grant that there isn't anyone better—right now you and me are face to face in a small room. The only way out of here is past me, Jonas. And a man like you knows better than to play the other fellow's game. This is *my* game, Jonas, and you couldn't come any closer to beating me at it than I could to whipping you at yours."

Hightower gave Longarm a grim smile. "Haven't you forgotten our friend Mr. Cane, Long? He remains behind you, you know."

"I haven't forgotten him, Jonas. But I don't think I have to worry about him. The only gun he's likely to have around is one of those in the drawers over there, and he can't reach them easy."

"Perhaps you misjudge him."

Longarm shrugged.

Cane spoke for the first time since the shock of seeing Longarm recognize Jonas Hightower stunned him into a frantic inaction. "I don't know what either one of you is talking about," he blustered. "Why, I..."

"Oh, hush, Sam."

"The money," Cane babbled on. "Those robbers..."

Longarm laughed. "Those poor ol' boys were washouts as bank robbers, weren't they, Sam? Came in here and found the damn time lock set. Couldn't get to the vault and likely never even knew about the little safe, though I bet they'd have been happy as a bunch of hogs in the sunshine to get whatever you had in there. But all they could see was that big ol' vault door and it shut tight. Even when they hauled off and pistol-whipped you, they couldn't get anyone to open it 'cause it wouldn't open until the time lock snapped. And then here came those boys from the mine, wandering up the street with guns in their hands. So those poor ol' boys cut and run and got themselves shot to pieces when they hadn't a cent to show for their troubles. Isn't that the way it went, Sam?"

Cane was trying to blubber out denials, but his tongue would not flap as fast as his brain kept trying to shove the words out.

"Of course it was," Longarm said. "Those old boys went hauling butt out the front door, and about then the time lock went.

"Outside there was all that excitement and gunfire and such, and in here there was just the three of you. And a wide-open bank vault that everybody thought had just been cleaned out by the gang they were shooting at.

"I got to give you credit for quick thinking, Sam," Longarm said. "You're a fellow as knows an opportunity when he sees one. You grabbed a pistol from one of the drawers and shot Walker Hardifer. He was a tightwad son of a bitch anyway, right? Probably paid you peanuts and rubbed it in about you owing him for your job to boot, right? And once you'd shot Hardifer you had to shoot the teller too. And once they were dead there was no reason in the world why you couldn't clean out the vault and stash it in a desk drawer or a wastebasket or something. Hell, everybody knew the bank had been robbed. So nobody was expecting to find any money *inside* the bank, nor look for any. It was a good plan, Sam. Quick. Real quick. I give you credit for that."

"But..."

"But how'd I know where it was? Sam, when you can't find something, maybe that's because it ain't there. This afternoon I found out that Chipeta, old Ouray's widow, has been in mourning ever since the old buzzard died. She's been sleeping on top of his grave and taking time out every now and then to chop another finger off. So the bank's money wasn't anywhere along the trail and couldn't have been buried in the grave either. About the only place it *could* be, then, was right in this here bank. It didn't take all that long to figure it out once I knew for sure where it *wasn't*."

Longarm heard the leather soles of the banker's shoes scrape on the hardwood flooring. He side-stepped behind the protection of the window wall, and Cane flew past him to sprawl on the floor at his feet.

The banker was the one trying to assault him, but Longarm's eyes remained fixed on Jonas Hightower. That was where the real danger lay.

Longarm was truly sorry that Hightower chose to use Sam Cane's attack as a diversion. The gentlemanly assassin reached under his coat.

176

"Don't," Longarm had time to warn.

Hightower was committed, though. He had apparently decided that he would live free or die here in this bank building.

Longarm pulled his Colt but held his fire, still hoping Hightower's hand would stop before it became necessary to shoot him.

The expert rifleman's choice of a personal protection weapon was almost laughably inadequate. He drew a tiny nickel-plated .32 revolver from a shoulder holster.

The little gun swung toward Longarm's belly, and the tall deputy fired.

The heavy .45 slug passed through Hightower's wrist, sending the pipsqueak revolver flying, and into the slender, white-haired man's chest. Hightower slumped back in his chair, and Longarm stopped himself barely in time to keep from triggering another round into him.

"Damn it, man, I wish you hadn't made me do that."

"So do I. Now." Hightower gave him a thin, apologetic smile and coughed. The cough brought flecks of blood to his lips, and already bright scarlet blood was staining the front of his shirt and spilling into his lap. "You've killed me, haven't you, Marshal?"

"Uh-huh. *Sam!* Lay right there. I don't feel like messing with you just now."

Cane sat on the floor looking like he wanted to cry.

"Someone will have heard the shot," Longarm said. "When they get here I'll send for the doctor."

Hightower shook his head. "It will do no good, but I thank you for the thought. And for the offer you made. I should have taken you up on it." He coughed again, and this time there was a great deal of blood reaching his mouth.

Cane looked away and began to vomit.

"What's the matter, Sam? Look worse when you didn't do it yourself?" Longarm felt nothing but disgust for the banker.

Jonas Hightower was becoming weaker. He and Longarm both knew that he had little more than seconds left to live.

"A favor, Marshal?"

"If I can."

"This...creature here." Hightower motioned toward Cane.

"Uh-huh."

"Make it known...I was associated...only professionally." He sighed, and blood dribbled out of his mouth and down his chin, spotting the immaculately white collar he wore. "Only that."

Longarm nodded. "I'll make sure they know."

The answer seemed to satisfy the handsome veteran of the Mormon wars. He closed his eyes, sighed once, and slipped away.

"Get up, Sam," Longarm snapped. He still had a prisoner to take care of.

Cane wiped his mouth and climbed shakily to his feet. He leaned against the desk. He looked pale and frightened. Longarm wondered how in the world a mouse like this had ever gotten up the nerve it took to murder two co-workers in cold blood. Probably, he thought, if the miserable little bastard had had time enough to think about it, he could not have done it.

Longarm shoved the Colt back into his holster and picked up the handcuffs he had hoped to put onto Jonas Hightower. He pulled Cane's wrists around behind his back and snapped the cuffs on.

"By the way, Cane, where did you hide the money?"

Cane shook his head.

"Look, you asshole, we're going to find it. You can at least save your wife the embarrassment of having strangers tear her house apart if you'll tell us where you put it."

"Cold bitch," Cane muttered. "Bad as her brother."

Longarm smiled. It was better, marginally better, than beating the shit out of the banker. He turned Cane around, took him by the collar, and began marching him toward the jail.

Chapter 21

"A very original fellow, your Mr. Cane." He took a mouthful of the stew the cafe was offering for lunch and made a face. "We found the money in a lard can, buried in the basement of the house. His wife claims she knew nothing about it, and I believe her. I hope you weren't thinking of charging her too."

"Not if you don't think I should," Jean said.

"No, I can't see her going along with it if she had any hint at all that Cane had murdered her own brother. So I'd suggest you leave her be. She'll have troubles enough without that too." He took another swallow of the greasy stew and washed it down with coffee.

He had to stifle a strong impulse to reach over and take Jean's hand. After all, they were in public here. He did not want to cause her any trouble either. But he had not seen her since shortly before dawn this morning. He certainly liked what he had seen of her then.

Something of what he was thinking must have reached his eyes, because she blushed and turned her head away.

Longarm changed the subject. "I must say we made that insurance man happy this morning. He stepped off the stage and found his company already off the hook for the loss."

"Did you find all of it?" she asked.

"All but two thousand dollars. And Jonas High-tower had eighteen hundred and some in his wallet, all but the small stuff in uncirculated hundreds. I think the insurance company will be mighty happy to make up that little bit of difference." He hesitated. "I think they will also be happy to pay a rather healthy recovery fee."

"Oh? I'm happy for you."

Longarm smiled. "As a matter of fact, ma'am, federal officers aren't allowed to accept rewards or reimbursement from outside sources. So I let the insurance man know that I was only there for the arrest part of it. The investigation was conducted by the town marshal here." He smiled. "After all, the bank robbery is out of my jurisdiction. I was just down here to deal with the Utes."

"Custis! You *didn't.*" The words were a protest, but the tone of voice told him that he would not have any trouble convincing her to accept the reward money. He hoped it would be enough to help her and her son get settled into a new life.

"Why don't I come by tonight and see if I can't persuade you?" he said.

She blushed again, but she sounded more than a little eager when she asked, "Does that mean you don't have to leave right away?"

"I'll have to wire the boss about what I'm up to, of course, but I can't hardly leave until my boots are fixed. Besides, I promised John Badger that I'd come out and spend some time with him. I think the government will accept the necessity for improved relations right now. So I'll be here until the cobbler is done with my boots, and then I'll be passing through again once I'm done at Los Pinos."

Jean smiled. "I think it might take several more days before Anton can get around to working on your boots. In fact, I am almost sure it will take that long."

181

"Tsk, tsk. Such terrible service in these small towns."

"*All* the servicing you've been getting here, Deputy?"

He grinned at her. "We'll discuss that tonight, Marshal."

Watch for

LONGARM WEST OF THE PECOS

seventy-fifth novel in the bold
LONGARM series from Jove

coming in March!